Catfish Pond
Woman

Paperback: 979-8-9879562-4-3
Ebook: 979-8-9879562-7-4

First paperback edition April 2024
Cover design: Elizabeth Golembiewski

"Catfish Pond Woman" was first published in *The Marr's Field Journal*

Printed by Mixam in the United States of America.

Red Rook Press
Box 870244
The University of Alabama
Tuscaloosa, AL 35487-0244

redrookpress.org

Catfish Pond Woman

a novel in stories

Bianca McCarty

Red Rook Press

A Letter for You
Kudzu Detention
Honky Tonk People
Illegal Bible Class
Dollar General

Jackson Siren Call
Snow
Tornado Fishing
Catfish Pond Woman
The Money
Five and a Half Feet Under

For all of my catfish pond women. You know who you are.

FIVE
AND A
HALF

FEET
UNDER

You stopped bothering with ghosts a long time ago. Even if they are real, they're of no concern to you.

At least the way you see it, if dead folks can float through walls and go wherever they want, why would they stay here?

Here. Where they're buried five and a half feet under because the gravedigger's a lazy son of a bitch. Where the dirt is packed with red clay and heat rots their lifeless skin quicker than a jackrabbit on cocaine. Where their graves will flood when the levee breaks again, and they'll go drifting through downtown like they did when they were alive, except this time filled with the cheapest chemicals the mortician could find.

And it's not *if* it's *when* because everything built down here falls apart—something dead folks understand just as well as anybody.

There are no ghosts in the Mississippi Delta.

It's why you've never been afraid when things go bump in the night. It's what you tell all your little brothers and sisters when they keep you up, hollering about the boogeyman, Dracula, and Tate Reeves all hiding under the bed.

You say to them, "Now what kinda business would the boogeyman have in Ass Crack, Mississippi? You think you're special enough for him to make a trip out to the middle of nowhere?"

Them kids know your argument makes sense, so they finally shut their mouths leaving you to stare at the ceiling and think of the only spirit you've ever known.

Your Uncle Bubba is a fresh ghost, taken to the Hereafter only a few days ago.

It was a combine accident that did him in. Ripped both his arms off like they were ears of corn and nearly popped his head like a watermelon.

The mortician had recommended a closed casket.

Well, he'd really said *it was up to y'all*, the family, to make the choice. But then he'd botched the autopsy and screwed up your Uncle Bubba's face even worse than the combine already had.

The mortician is sort of a jack-of-all trades, meaning he's also the medical examiner and the butcher.

When you and your MawMaw had gone over to the butcher shop/funeral home/medical examiner's office, the mortician—still in his butcher's apron—had at least offered a discount for your Uncle Bubba's missing eyes and nose.

"Well, I can't exactly charge you full price for an eyeless and nose-less body," the mortician had said.

"No, you couldn't," your MawMaw had responded. "It wouldn't be honest, and our Lord hates the dishonest."

He'd nodded seriously, as one does when God is invoked, then sent you on your way with a stiff smile and a photocopy of a "Sorry for Your Loss" sympathy card.

On the way out, you'd tossed the sheet of paper back and forth between your hands, wondering if times were really so hard that the mortician couldn't afford a real card from the drugstore.

"He coulda at least printed it in color," you'd said.

MawMaw's only response was, "Stop being ungrateful."

Being grateful as ever, you push the cart behind MawMaw as she shuffles down the aisle of Goodwill. She's piling it up with more things than the entire extended family could ever need, much less now that your Uncle Bubba's gone. The two of them had been the sole residents of her double wide trailer ever since Pappy kicked the bucket.

MawMaw holds up a pair of woolen tights with a hole right in the crotch.

"Won't these do nicely for you come wintertime?"

You give her a look. Then remember how grateful you're being.

"Yeah, they're nice, MawMaw," you say with great effort. "Would probably be good for church."

"I'm glad you like 'em, baby." She inspects them again. "Wait a minute! They got a hole in 'em! Why the hell didn't you say something, girl? Tryin' to embarrass your MawMaw at church by lookin' ragged? Shame on you!"

You don't say anything. You've learned that it's usually better not to open your mouth when MawMaw gets to ranting about shame and holey tights. She keeps moving down the secondhand rack of clothes, talking and talking, but not to you or anyone. Her blue-gray hair is sticking up in the back, the only indication that she might be even a little upset that her son is dead.

You're acutely aware that y'all are at the Goodwill for one reason, one that your MawMaw is skillfully avoiding. That reason being your Uncle Bubba's corpse laying on a slab meant for slicing steaks with not a scrap to wear for his funeral. You know that naked frame of skin and bones isn't really your uncle anymore—whatever it is that made him Uncle Bubba is long gone. And if he's a ghost now, you know he didn't stick around Ass Crack. You'd like to think he'd at least check on you before he went, if God or the Devil gave him the time, but Uncle Bubba was always forgetful.

You know he wouldn't have given a rat's ass about what he was buried in. He used to say a whole bunch of crazy shit about his body being ground up for fertilizer or thrown in the Mississippi river when he died. But your MawMaw would never allow such a barbaric burial, especially since the mortician needs the business. Folks just aren't dying like they used to—at least that's what he says. Sometimes you wonder if times are really hard enough to justify the photocopied sympathy card. Every time he sees you, he hands you a business card and says some cryptic bullshit about "young people not being invincible" and to "keep him in mind just in case."

Your cousin, Bob Joe, used to apprentice on the butcher side of things. Though word on the street is that he did a few autopsies when the mortician was out of town on business. He never said what that business was, and you must admit you were curious, but you know better than to pry into the innerworkings of the departed. Believe it or not, they're real sensitive about the whole *being dead* thing.

Your MawMaw has finally found a suit for the funeral, among other things, and now the two of you stand in the checkout line next to a woman you've never seen before. Which is odd because you've seen everyone in this town at the Goodwill too much.

"You from around these parts?" your MawMaw asks. She's a real Southerner in the way that she can't resist talking to somebody. "Because I know everyone in this town like the back of my hand and I ain't never set eyes on you before."

"Aw nah, I'm just passin' through," replies the woman. "Fixin' to head over the bridge to Louisiana."

"Ain't that nice. You know, my Daddy helped build that bridge back in the day."

You're pretty sure that's a bold-faced lie, but the out-of-towner seems impressed.

"Wow, ain't that something! Y'all girls out shopping for a special occasion?"

"Oh well, we've got a funeral coming up tomorrow," MawMaw replies casually, like it's another just another errand she has to run.

"Bless y'all. I'm so sorry about your loss," says the out-of-towner. "Were you close to the deceased?"

Right as you say "yes" your MawMaw says "no," and you're left staring at each other in the Goodwill checkout line like two deer in headlights. It's a skin-crawling moment for the two of you, so it must be even worse for the out-of-towner.

Yet, she launches into another sentence like nothing happened, the polite smile on her face never fading. That's Southern ladies for you. You almost have to admire it.

"You can get such good stuff for cheap here, don't y'all think?" the woman says.

Your MawMaw nods. "I got me some real classy stuff this time, I'd say. Good for the funeral."

"When I go to funerals, I usually just wear the same black dress. That's a real interesting suit you've got there," she says, and points to the khaki suit in MawMaw's arms. In the South, "interesting" is a nice way of saying "horrific," and you can't help but agree with her. Your MawMaw was never known for her fashion sense.

"That for your husband?" she continues, smile still wide as the river.

"Oh no, this is for the body."

A pause more painful than when you broke your nose falling off MawMaw's roof.

Then the out-of-towner says, "Well...I suppose he won't be needing it again."

Now you're at the funeral in a hand-me-down black dress, head spinning because time has been moving strange ever since Uncle Bubba died. It skips like a rock on the surface of the drainage pond out behind the school, leaving you as confused as MawMaw waking up from her naps.

You don't remember getting ready or driving to the church, but evidently, you're here now and you've got to be polite to all the people who came out to say goodbye to your uncle. It seems to you that politeness is the entire point of a funeral. Uncle Bubba wouldn't —couldn't—care about any of this shit. And if he was watching from above or below, you knew he'd want to ask you why the hell you didn't just feed him to the pigs like he'd wanted. In return, you'd ask him why he had to die in the heat of the summer because under this old black dress, you're sweating rivers.

Even in the semi air-conditioned church, it's hot as Hell—which is where some people think Uncle Bubba is going. Everyone is fanning themselves with the programs bearing Uncle Bubba's face as you, MawMaw, your Daddy, your Ma, and all your siblings stand rigid in the front pew. You've been trying not to look at the closed casket directly before your eyes. Instead, you choose to stare at your shoes and breathe in the scent of the white lilies and forget-me-nots adorning the sanctuary. The fragrance mixes with the earthy scent of so many people sweating together in one room.

All of Ass Crack, Mississippi is here, even though you know most of them didn't care for your Uncle Bubba. But Southerners are hypocrites, so the church is damn packed. Third and fourth cousins have come out of the woodwork for ole Bubba, who had been notorious in his own right, you suppose.

Your Uncle Billy, Bubba's only brother that survived the crop-duster crash, gives the eulogy. Your Ma refused to do it because she hates talking in front of people. Plus, she couldn't get up there and lie about how much she loved her little brother.

Uncle Billy doesn't look much like Uncle Bubba. He's more tan, more weathered, the type to be out picking soybeans in the hot sun.

And from this disjointed eulogy, you can tell that Billy doesn't read even half as much as Uncle Bubba did.

He clears his throat and straightens the freshly ironed pair of mourning overalls he's wearing underneath his suit jacket.

"Bubba was a real piece of work," he begins.

"Amen," says the congregation.

"By golly, he was a real piece of shit sometimes."

"Amen."

"Always talkin' 'bout all these crazy ideas like democracy and equal rights. And Lord our Bubba couldn't carry a tune in a bucket. But that sure didn't stop him from singing loud as all hell at every church service."

There is polite, shrill laughter from the congregation. You want to pop some of them on the head.

Billy starts to get serious here, lowering his head to shield his face from a church full of people he knows far too well.

"Even after he stopped going, I'd catch him singing the hymns we'd sung that Sunday like he knew somehow. And I'd find the Bible open in his bedroom with notes all in the margins. I never said anything because y'all know how Bubba could be. A real piece of work."

You're keenly aware that you should be crying right now. Your Ma is, even though she and Uncle Bubba never got along a day in their lives.

But even as you watch Billy grit his teeth to keep the tears from flowing, your eyes are dry. You can't help but feel a little heartless.

"But he was *our* Bubba. Shit, he was my baby brother. And I'm sorry for my language, God, but even He knows that Bubba would have loved to hear me cussin' at a funeral." He takes a deep breath. "I don't know why that wildfire got him. I don't understand it either. Don't think I ever will. Of course, y'all know I've been tryin' to contact his spirit but, my God, he won't talk to me. Why won't he just say something? Jesus Fuckin' Christ, how could he just go on and get?

Without even a sign? He was such a fuckin' piece of shit. Oh Lord, can I sit down now?"

Billy doesn't wait for an answer. He just tears down the aisle and out the door. One of the deacons follows him, his comb-over flopping as he runs. The rest of the church sits in a silence so heavy you can actually feel it weighing on your shoulders.

Then the choir starts up a rendition of Amazing Grace and everyone begins singing.

And, bam, the funeral's over and you're standing outside the church shaking hands and nodding at all the sympathy. It's hot. You're sweating and your brain hurts, fogging up like the time you and your siblings all came down with meningitis.

When you feel a light tap on your shoulder you nearly jump out of your skin.

"Uncle Bubba?" you ask, whipping around.

"Nah," comes a familiar voice. "Just Colt."

Your half-brother stands before you in a black jacket far too small for him. Typical. Ever since last summer, Colton's been growing too fast for clothes and Daddy's paycheck. The ladies in your Ma's bible study call him "cornfed."

Colton shifts uncomfortably, tugging at the cuffs of his sleeves.

"What?" you ask as a bead of sweat drips down your face. You know something's wrong—well, something other than your Uncle Bubba in rigor mortis—because your Ma always sends Colton to deal with you whenever she doesn't feel like doing the dealing herself.

"Well, look it's just...everyone knows you're real upset about Bubba, and you know we get it, and obviously we're all torn up about him getting killed in that paper shredder but..."

It's getting even hotter as Colton trails on and on like the Mississippi flowing down from Minnesota.

"Just spit it out," you blurt.

"Okay, yeah, it's just that Ma said to tell you that you need to quit acting like you are 'cause you're freaking people out."

"What?"

Colton shifts his eyes to the ground. "Ma thinks you outta have tried harder to cry."

They bury Uncle Bubba at the crossroads.

He lies five and a half feet under the red dirt in the southernmost corner of the local cemetery.

Only you, MawMaw, and Billy are there to watch the casket lower into the ground. The rest of the town has their excuses for not being here.

"Oh, deary me," they'd said. "Look at the time... I've got to go milk the cows, and there's a casserole in the oven...my goodness, how unfortunate. Well, bless y'all's hearts, okay?"

Your Ma couldn't be there on account of a grief-induced fainting spell. Of course, your Daddy had to care for her, and all the kiddos stayed back to help him.

You try not to judge them, but you're from the South—it's in your nature.

The gravedigger buries Uncle Bubba the old-fashioned way. He uses a single shovel and some elbow grease despite being older than the dirt he's digging. The process is excruciatingly slow, but as you said earlier, time doesn't work the same anymore.

Billy's a mess, weeping into your MawMaw's shoulder. You've never seen a man cry like that before. Still, your eyes are dry as you burn up in the black funeral dress. Sweat drips from your hairline into your eyes, the salt stinging. Inside the casket, Uncle Bubba wears the world's worst Goodwill khaki suit. You know he hates it. You hate it for him.

Once the dirt is finally packed, you place a bouquet of flowers on the grave. Queen Ann's Lace.

"Where'd you get them weeds, child?" MawMaw asks.

"Side of the road," you mutter. "They were Uncle Bubba's favorite."

For once, MawMaw doesn't push it, just holds Billy as he cries, as if she could absorb his pain.

Uncle Bubba's grave bears the inscription, *"When you go through deep waters, I will be with you… When you walk through the fire of oppression, you will not be burned up; the flames will not consume you."*

He didn't choose it, but out of all the Bible verses, he would have liked this one.

Atop the grave, the Queen Ann's Lace wilt in the heat, the stems crushed from your iron grip. Their blossoms remind you of all the times you'd driven down the highway with your Uncle Bubba and seen those flowers coating the median in white, almost like snow.

"You oughta see snow one day," he'd said over the roaring A.C. and blasting rock music. "But if you don't, it's a lot like those flowers—Queen Ann's Lace."

Now that Uncle Bubba is five and a half feet under, thus no longer occupying his old room in MawMaw's trailer, you move in instead.

Your Ma doesn't tell you until you get home from the funeral.

She sits propped up in her and Daddy's bed. Her face is puffy and red. She looks you up and down and says, "That dress don't flatter you much."

Your expression remains flat.

"Your Daddy and I think you ought to go live with MawMaw now that Bubba's no longer with us."

You don't say anything. How could you? You've got ten million other siblings and for some reason she chose you.

"She might get lonely, you know?" your Ma says, and inspects you like she always does. "Go ahead and pack up now."

Everyone knows MawMaw needs no one but herself.

You turn to leave but stop on your way out. Without turning to look at her, you ask your Ma one question, "Why me?"

"You're the oldest."

"But I'm not. You've got Colton and Isaiah."

Your Ma doesn't say anything. You know she's thinking about how Colton and Isaiah aren't your Daddy's children, how she had them out of wedlock when she was barely older than you—she'd just gotten her driver's license. You still have another year to wait. In Biblical terms, which seem to be the parameters for everything down here, your brothers are *illegitimate.*

As for you, you're legitimate and a girl, therefore the bearer of all the responsibility no one else wants.

"I don't have an answer for you, baby," your Ma says. "Go pack up."

So, you do just that.

That night you sleep in a cot in the center of Uncle Bubba's bedroom. He used to call it a study, but it was actually a room with a lot of books stacked up against the walls. All his things are just as he left them, messier than the town after the big tornado came through last spring. He'd left a Bible open on the floor and a few beer bottles piled in the corner. The room still smells like him, a scent you can only describe as Uncle Bubba.

You don't sleep. How could you?

You lie awake praying that Uncle Bubba's ghost will come back for just a moment, for just a second and a half.

DOLLAR
GENERAL

In the summer, time is like a horseshoe lake—pinched off from the Mississippi until the school year comes again and you find yourself back in its strong flow. Fighting the river is useless. You've known that since you were a child. If you're stupid enough to try and swim it, you deserve the brown water flooding your lungs and dragging you into the deep. Well, that's what your Daddy says.

It seems that you've reached the end of the horseshoe lake and summer is winding to a close. So, here comes August, burning its way into the Mississippi Delta and thrusting all them kids, including you, back into school. The murderous heat boils your brains, clearing out everything you learned last year. At least the school cafeteria has air conditioning.

You're not saying it was a good summer. Nah, it was a summer with your MawMaw and without your Uncle Bubba. You didn't see anyone but the two of them for most of it—MawMaw hollering in your face and Bubba in your dreams, still torn up from the lawnmower accident that killed him. As much as you'd expected a real-life waking visit, his ghost has stayed elusive, probably off in New York City by now. As for your Ma, she seems to be following her brother's example of seemingly wanting nothing to do with you.

In summers past, there had been weekly pool visits when Colton was off work and expensive powdered lemonade on paydays. Sure, water at the Ass Crack public pool reeked of chlorine and gave your littlest brother salmonella once, but it was far better than roasting to death at home. When you tired of swimming, you and Isaiah would ride your bikes a few miles to the public library a town over so he could play video games on the computers, and you could find something to read. At first, you'd just enjoyed the air conditioning and watching Isaiah play the games, his knobby fingers tapping on the greasy keyboard. Isaiah had a decisive and interesting way of doing things, even if it was just beating whatever games the library didn't have blocked. Eventually, as is typical of older brothers, he'd grown tired of you being there.

"Get," he'd said. "Go do something else."

So, you'd migrate to the kid section and work your way through all the chapter books they had. By the end of that summer, you were left with only the science books filled with intricate diagrams and words like *evolution* and *thermodynamics*. Your Uncle Bubba helped you read them until your Ma caught the two of you sitting on MawMaw's porch whispering about chimpanzee DNA.

As for this summer, there was none of that. No pool, no books, no fancy lemonade powder. Well, there were a few books here and there, but only ones your MawMaw picked out. Most of this summer was spent digging up weeds in MawMaw's garden, wrangling cattle, and building fences in the burning Mississippi sun. You'd only passed out from heat exhaustion once or twice, though, so you couldn't complain too much—even if the whole moving in with MawMaw thing is kind of shit.

Yet today you're living large because MawMaw let you take the tractor down to the Dollar General for some school supplies for you and chicken gizzards for her. This year you've got a bigger budget— twenty whole dollars — because you're taking all two of the honors classes offered.

"We got a regular Einstein in the family, don't we?" your MawMaw said last Sunday after service. You're pretty sure she only goes to church to brag on her grandbabies afterwards. She doesn't brag on you much, probably because you're no good at baking cornbread and you've only shot two deer. Still, that troublesome mind of yours gives you a little something. No one says it, but you've got a quicker mind than most of the other cousins since illiteracy and diabetes run in the family.

You park the tractor out front of the Dollar General and nod at all the folks you know in the parking lot. Your Ma always says politeness is a virtue. You have the twenty-dollar bill tucked in your Walmart sports bra, right against your heart. As much as you love the Dollar

General—nearly as much as Waffle House—you know it attracts the thieving types, men with shifty eyes and rat tails scraping the floor. You aren't the thieving type yourself, at least not after the old McDonald's manager sliced off a boy's ear for stealing the toilet paper out of the bathroom. The judge called it self-defense.

As you walk through the door of the Dollar General, both the heat and the smell smack you in the face. Your eyes start to water and you immediately start sweating like a pig, but hey, that's the Dollar General experience.

The cashier is lying on the counter, shirtless and dripping, nursing an equally sweaty Bud Light.

"A.C.'s out," he calls to you without even lifting his head.

"I figured as much."

As for the smell, it is best described as rotten eggs. It's a pervasive kind of stench and will certainly linger in your hair for days afterwards, no matter how raw MawMaw scrubs your scalp.

MawMaw's chicken gizzards are behind the counter in a freezer you're praying hasn't gone out. And that means you've got to go talk to the half-naked, half-drunk cashier sprawled out for all to see.

It's usually a girl working the register. You think she's your age, or somewhere close to it, because you swear you've seen her in the halls at school. You remember her because her hair is dyed black in a town where most folks are trying to be blond. She never talks to anyone, even when they ask her direct questions. Instead, she just points and glares, and you find yourself wishing that you had the strength to be mean like that. Your Ma says she's a good-for-nothing, but people say that about Isaiah constantly and she still loves him.

As you observe the cashier, you think that he might be related to you, because he sure seems illiterate.

MawMaw says now that you're a young lady, you've got to handle social interactions with delicacy and grace. You don't think that this particular situation requires either. The Dollar General rarely does.

"Hey, you," is what you say to the cashier because you can't remember his name for love nor money.

He doesn't respond. You start to wonder if he's drunker than you initially thought. And you don't want to touch him because he's a sweaty, hairy man, but you've got to get those damn gizzards or MawMaw will whoop your ass. So, you poke him with one of the empty beer bottles scattered at your feet.

"Excuse me," you say more insistently. "I need to get me some gizzards."

The cashier opens one vomit-green colored eye, peering at you apprehensively.

"*Gizzards*," you insist.

"Damn, girl, give a poor soul a minute to breathe," he grumbles at you.

You don't say anything. Uncle Bubba used to say that silence is a powerful thing.

"*Fine*," says the cashier. "I'm going."

He rolls off the counter and walks about two steps to the gizzard freezer. You want to say something snarky, like, "Now, was that so hard?" but your Maw-Maw said never to talk sassy to men you don't know very well, because men you don't know very well are the types to kill you over next to nothing.

The cashier hands you the plastic bag of gizzards, icy cold against your hot skin.

"Thank you," you say.

He grunts in response.

You roll your eyes and head deeper into the store towards the school supplies. The farther you walk the more intense both the smell and the heat get. Your stomach begins to turn, and your eyes begin to water yet, you press on. Bugs begin to swarm around your face, sticking in the sweat collecting at your temple. You swat them away with your one free hand. Your palm collides with the wings of wasps and bees. These are bugs you stopped fearing long ago. Sure, the doctor says you're deathly allergic, but what does he know?

Since it's Dollar General, absolutely nothing is organized as it should be. Your MawMaw says that whoever designed the place "didn't have the sense they were born with." The aisles are cramped and non-sensical, towering over you like the tallest buildings in downtown Jackson.

Jackson.

In Jackson they have cellular telephones that flip open and have a glossy shine to them and get hot against your ear if you talk too long. But in Ass Crack the telephone is still tethered to the wall with those looping cords Isaiah manages to stretch all the way to his room while he's, "talking up the ladies," as Colton puts it.

Once you asked your Ma why y'all don't have a cellular telephone if all the people in the cities do. She'd said, "Cellular ain't cheap."

Your ears are starting to feel hot, as if you were rich enough to talk for hours on a cellular telephone. The air has grown hazy with heat, blurring the edges of the shelves, and making your eyes play tricks on you. You swear you see a large, looming deer standing over the spiral notebooks, but when you blink, it's gone.

Nevertheless, you're in the school supplies aisle now and you've got to choose what color to get for each school subject. It's one of the most important decisions of the year, probably your whole life, so you sit down in the aisle to make it. The linoleum floor is cool against your sweaty thighs. Over the egg stench, you can smell the delicious scent of fresh paper, full of possibility and excitement. You open your mouth to breathe it in, tasting new beginnings on the back of your tongue.

You've decided that red is definitely English and green is Mississippi History, though blue is difficult to pin down. Perhaps Math or Bible class?

As you're pondering this, you feel something ice cold press against your elbow. Instinctively, your hands ball into fists readying to punch someone's lights out. You whip your head around.

There's nothing there.

Your blood is starting to pump quicker than usual, and the gizzards are thawing way too fast, but you've got pencils and erasers to get before you can escape the grasp of the Dollar General.

In the haze, you swear you can see figures watching you. They're in the shape of the ladies from church. You know they're thinking about your scraggly haircut, and how shit your vegetables did at the county fair, especially compared to your little sister's turnip the size of her head.

Every time you close your eyes and open them again the figures disappear. Taking their taunting glances with them, they leave you sweltering hot and unsettled. You're usually not the type to let menacing shadows get to you, but you've been oddly jumpy ever since Uncle Bubba died.

To hell with the pencils and erasers. Walmart will have some.

When you go to stand up, it's like all the blood rushes out of your head. Suddenly your stomach is doing the cartwheels your arms and legs could never figure out how to do. You fall to your knees as a wave of nausea hits. The gizzards and notebooks, slick with your sweat, slip out of your hands and onto the floor. As puke rises in your throat, all you can think is how embarrassing it would be to throw up in the goddamn

Dollar General school supplies aisle. It's the kind of thing your Uncle Bubba would have never let you live down.

Motivated by this, you stumble towards the back of the store. You throw open the "employees only" bathroom door, wracked with chills despite the heat.

Of course, the bathroom's disgusting, but no worse than the one you used to share with all your siblings. You're powerless to stop your collapse onto the grimy tile floor. You brace yourself against the cool ceramic of the toilet seat, unable to care whose ass has touched it. Your mind swims, twirling like the psychedelic swirls from the anti-drug videos at school.

The Kraft mac and cheese you had for lunch ends up in the toilet bowl, and somehow, so does a small black wasp.

Exhausted, you lift your head to the mirror. There, in bright red lipstick, is written,

Abandon all hope ye who enter here

ILLEGAL
BIBLE
CLASS

You try not to use the bathroom in between classes because that's when all the freshmen are holed up in the big stall moonshining like Al Capone. They aren't subtle about it, of course, they're freshmen. Their specialty is prison toilet wine. They've been peddling in the parking lot after school ever since one of them did time in the Central Mississippi Correctional Facility down in Jackson. You're not exactly sure how they've managed to fool with the plumbing and keep the janitor from coming in there after school, but some of those kids got bigwig connections to the Reverend who teaches Bible class third period. In Ass Crack, the Reverend has more power than the Governor of Mississippi.

You walked into the big stall—moonshine headquarters—on accident once. You'd been dog tired from the night before, studying for that very Bible class. When you swung the door open, the freshmen scared the shit out of you because they were armed to the teeth with shanks and hunting rifles they kept slung over their backs.

"The hell you playin' at?" one of them snapped, pulling a sharpened butter knife out of the pocket of his cutoff jean shorts. The blade had glinted in the fluorescent lighting, bright as a carnival. There were about four of them in there at the time, only one of which was even allowed to be in the girl's bathroom.

"I ain't playin' at nothing," you'd said. "I just gotta piss."

"That code for something?" the girl sneered, crossing her tanned arms over her tank top.

"Have you forgotten where we are?" you laughed. "This is the girl's bathroom before it's Al Capone's hideout."

"Who's Al? Some kinda cop? You know snitches get stitches."

"None of y'all got the sense you were born with," you'd said, and marched out of the stall because you really did have to piss.

Ever since then you only go to the bathroom during class. You usually get away with asking during English or Math, but Bible class is damn strict about bodily functions. Things only got more difficult when the whole school lost bathroom privileges since too many folks were setting off the fire alarms with cigarette smoke. Now they lock the bathrooms in between classes, and only the Reverend has the key. Sometimes he don't unlock them for an entire day and you're pretty sure it's because he gets some sick enjoyment out of watching all y'all squirm in your seats because you haven't peed in eight hours.

The boys are lucky; they just unzip their bootcut jeans and piss outside in the grass next to the gym.

As for the girls, you're pretty sure being denied a bathroom is some sort of violation of your civil rights. But then you remember you're in Mississippi so, civil rights, especially those of good-for-nothing teenagers, aren't of particular concern.

This is only made worse by the fact that the Reverend doesn't like you one lick.

The obvious reason for his loathing is your Uncle Bubba and your half-brothers Colton and Isaiah. Uncle Bubba questioned him too much, of course, and the hate the Reverend harbors hasn't faded even after Bubba died in that tornado. As for Colton and Isaiah, their only crime was being the Reverend's sons.

It took you far too long to figure that out, though everyone else in town has known for years. They just don't talk about it. After you put it together, a few things began to make sense: why your family always sits in the back during service, why Isaiah has the Reverend's hellfire eyes while Colton got his wonky left ear, and how both boys inherited his booming preacher voice, though they were still only teenagers. Back when you lived with your Ma, the two of them fighting was like spiritual warfare. Those voices would echo down the halls, snapping you back to the sermon the day before.

You shudder to think of the Reverend and your Ma doing whatever they had to do to make a baby. You know it had to be something real unholy because even Uncle Bubba wouldn't tell you where you and your siblings had come from, and he told you everything you know.

When you walk into Bible class, you keep your head down. The Reverend is right at the front as usual, thumping his Bible before the tardy bell has even rung.

You take your seat right in the back, where Colton and Isaiah had been forced to sit when they took this class a couple years ago, though they'd opted to skip most days to go smoke in the parking lot. "Only the Satanic types sit in the back of Bible class," the Reverend had said. But you never bothered to move forward because you know moving forward would just remind the Reverend of what he'd done to your Ma to get her pregnant.

So, you stay in your desk between the girl with dyed black hair and the town's one homosexual.

Well, you suppose you're not completely sure if he's a homosexual or not, because even when you squint your eyes and look real hard, you see nothing that exactly gives it away. It's mostly the football team that calls him a homosexual, but if you think about it, the football team has almost never been right about anything.

After the one of the Reverend's more sin-focused sermons, you'd asked your Ma, "what's a homosexual?" She'd gotten all flustered and told you it was when men want to see other men "nekked." That surprised you, because the way the Reverend had been talking, you'd thought the homosexuals must be going around shooting puppies and pissing on American flags. You guessed that there really wasn't all that much wrong with men being "nekked" together and that everyone in town, especially all them football boys, seemed to be shitting it over nothing.

You understand why the alleged homosexual has chosen a seat in the back of the class, far away from the Reverend with his fire eyes and brimstone breath. His gaze has a way of burning right through a person. Sometimes you get the sense that he can see right through your clothes.

As for the black-haired girl, you aren't sure what her deal is, only that she works at the Dollar General and runs with the toilet wine crowd.

But the three of y'all make a good team, bound by a silent pact while the Reverend goes on and on about Satan, staring right at y'all in the back of the classroom.

Today's class is about the role of women in the church and society. Clearly, the Reverend is absolutely buzzing to talk about this topic, because he starts his rant the second after the bell rings, stopping only to reprimand whoever was foolish enough to be late to Bible class.

You don't listen, because why would you? It's nothing more than a man's idea of womanhood.

Once upon a time, you and your Uncle Bubba had been riding around in his truck searching for wild onions and Queen Ann's Lace on the side of the road. He'd been driving, of course, and you'd been hanging out the passenger side window, mouth wide open to see if you could catch any bugs. The radio had been blaring Uncle Bubba's heathen music—Duran Duran.

Then all of the sudden, Uncle Bubba had switched off the cassette player, catching you so off guard you'd lost the lovebug you'd captured between your teeth.

"You," Uncle Bubba had said in a serious voice.

"Yeah?" You'd pulled your head back inside the cabin, shaking hair from your eyes.

"I gotta tell you something that I think at least one person in your life ought to tell you."

"If it's the 'don't go swimming in the Mississippi River, the current's stronger than you think, you'll drown' talk, Pappy told me all that in kindergarten."

Uncle Bubba shook his head.

"No, I gotta tell you this: never let a man tell you what to do."

You considered that for a second before you'd replied, "Ain't you a man? And ain't you just tell me what to do?"

Uncle Bubba smiled his half toothless smile.

"Now that's kinda attitude I like to see."

That's what you're thinking about as the Reverend makes himself red-faced over shoulders showing in church and the epidemic of bellybutton piercings. He's up there huffing and puffing like the Big Bad wolf. Hell, he's got to be getting light-headed, but he isn't stopping. You don't think even Jesus coming back in a G-string and cowboy hat could make that man quit.

"It's a pure and utter disgrace!" the Reverend shouts. "A pure and utter disgrace how the young women of this generation conduct themselves. Wearin' next to nothing and knockin' boots with boys at the drop of a hat!"

He looked right at the black-haired girl when he said that. She makes no indication that she's even noticed. You're wondering what's so bad about kicking folks while wearing cowboy boots, because those are the best kicking shoes this side of the Mississippi.

But the Reverend moves on like a tornado tearing through town. You think he's going to make himself sick. And, of course, he's the reason why this damn school has such a strict dress code: no shoulders, no ankles, no elbows, no nothing.

You've heard all this horse shit already, so you stare at the whiteboard behind him and zone out. This is a small exercise in freedom as you've recently realized the power of your mind. No, not its power for doing schoolwork or lucid dreaming. Rather, you'd realized that you can think about whatever you want, and no one can stop you. In a town where no one has a lick of privacy, only your thoughts are truly yours.

Fuck, shit, bitch, toilet moonshine, 'nekked' men— your brain runs wild, and you relish in the little bit of defiance against the Reverend and his Bible thumping ways.

Yet you can't help but hear some of the Reverend's hollering. He is louder than your thoughts, probably louder than God Himself.

"It's a shame what this nation has come to!" He spits all over the first row. "We used to be a Godly people, 'one nation under God!' Until demons took hold of our government and pushed God the Father to the side! Disgraceful! Disgraceful!" He's shaking now.

The Reverend's words have got you thinking, which is exactly the opposite of what he wants.

You remember all you learned in American History last year. All that talk about separation of church and state. Before you can stop yourself, you blurt out,

"Ain't this illegal?"

Your peers stare at you. The Reverend's face grows impossibly red and his hellfire eyes flash at you. But for some reason, you keep running your mouth.

"I'm just saying that separation of church and state is a thing we learned about in history last year. And ain't this a public school? Which would make a Bible class like this...illegal?"

The Reverend takes a deep breath, and you brace for impact.

Long story short, he makes you sit in the hallway for the rest of class.

The linoleum is cold against your ass, pressing hard into your butt bone. Somehow, you're still sweaty. Boys give you looks as they shamble outside to piss, but you ignore them. It's easy to ignore boys when you've been doing it all your life.

You let your mind drift off until the bell rings and all the other students come spilling out of class. One of the girls who sits in the front of Bible class and bats her eyes at the Reverend goes sprinting down the hall, bathroom key in hand. A herd of other girls follows her, because they know this is their only chance to piss today.

You're in no hurry to get to your next class so, you sit for a while and watch the bustle around you.

"Ahem," comes a voice you don't recognize.

You look up, making eye contact with the black-haired girl. Beneath all the hair, her eyes are mud brown with a sort of smoky quality to them.

"Yes?" you say, a bit confused because she's never talked to you before.

"I liked that thing you said," she says in a raspy voice.

"It was dumb. All it did was land me in time-out."

"Nah, it wasn't dumb. It was fucking cool. It was *punk rock*."

You don't know what punk rock means, but you're afraid to tell the black-haired girl that. You just say, "thank you," real polite, and stand up to go.

But the black-haired girl follows you down the hallway, telling you how much she hates that godforsaken Bible class because the Reverend calls all good music Satanic.

You're wrestling with the door of your locker when she says, "My name's Tallulah."

You look at her and nod.

"Don't go spreading this, but if you ever want some moonshine, I can get you a discount."

She winks one of her silt-colored eyes and disappears into the rush of the hallway.

You think your Uncle Bubba would have liked Tallulah and her Satanic music.

SNOW

The Reverend's on the radio talking in a real low voice, something about the end times, something about snow.

"Hold your women and children and livestock close, warriors of the Lord. 'Cause all y'all know what Deuteronomy 23:1 says, 'the Devil lurks in the cold, he lurks in the snow.'"

It's something you've never seen before because you're a genuine, real-deal Mississippian—sweaty most days, just how it should be.

Here, summer rages like Katrina all them years ago, leaving sunburns and mosquito bites across your thick Delta skin like constellations. Still, it's a rage you know, like MawMaw every few months when she tries to quit smoking— it hasn't ever taken— and the ole boys at school when they lose a football game.

As for snow, you've only ever seen it on the Hallmark Channel around Christmas time, when all the movies are about an average looking brunette lady and the squarest man you've ever seen. When they finally kiss, those little white flakes fall out of the sky and sit delicately in their hair like the fairies you used to believe in. MawMaw always made you cover your eyes when they started necking, but you peeked through your fingers like Jezebel surely would have. You're definitely going to Hell for that one.

You have to admit, you're skeptical about this snow. Because come every winter, everyone and their mama likes to talk a lotta shit about all the blizzards we're supposed to be getting, all the sleet and winds stronger than Goliath himself. They'll talk about how sad it is, all the homeless people freezing down in Jackson, about how they build fires in trashcans and sleep under benches by the Governor's Mansion downtown while the governor himself sits all warm and cozy in that giant white house. They talk about Jackson like Sodom and Gomorrah, a place full of city-folk with not a God-fearing bone in their bodies. They gave your third cousin Willie Joe a lotta shit for going to college right in the belly of that city, because, "why wasn't Delta State good enough for you Willie Joe? You better than us?" Willie Joe had told them to go straight to Hell and kiss the Devil's ass. Uncle Bubba hollered laughing when Willie Joe had said that at the bi-annual family barbeque. Everyone in town comes. They're probably family somehow, even if you can't trace it.

"Ain't that a real writer's mouth folks?" he'd said. "I think we got us the next Faulkner, the next Welty!"

No one else but Willie Joe seemed to really understand what he'd been talking about. She'd smiled bright and true at those words. You didn't know Willie Joe very well before she skipped town, but after those words left her mouth, you loved her something fierce—she was second only to your Uncle Bubba.

Uncle Bubba thought snow was something every little redneck boy or girl outta see at least once in their lives. He didn't pray much, but when he did, he asked God that you would see snow sooner rather than later.

You flip to the weather channel to see if the Reverend's just talking the same kinda shit everyone in this state does, or if Uncle Bubba's prayer might actually be answered now that he was dead as a doornail because of that wildfire. How typical of God.

"Now y'all," said the weatherman. *"I know it sounds crazy, but I'm a scientist, and this is what the science says."*

MawMaw says not to believe scientists, but she still listens to the weather every morning.

"We got a seventy percent chance of snow, y'all. That means get some gas for your generators, 'cause we all know the power lines go down at the drop of a hat."

If you close your eyes, you can imagine how all the folks listening to the radio in their own homes are reacting to that news. Probably a lotta shrieking from the mamas, indifference from the daddies, and shouts of joy from all the little bits.

"MawMaw!" you holler, switching off the radio and pacing round the little kitchen of MawMaw's double wide trailer. The floors are creaky and plastic feeling through your house shoes and thick hunting socks. Your MawMaw is a big fan of yellow so, the whole damn kitchen is either egg yolk, sunflower, or pollen colored. When Pappy was alive, he used to insist on wearing sunglasses every time he ate at the little table for two shoved in between the fridge and the stove. "It's too damn bright," he'd say every few minutes. "How's a fella supposed to enjoy his dinner in the goddamn neon piss-kitchen?"

"MAWMAW!" you holler again. Ole bat probably forgot her hearing trumpet at church again. When she doesn't answer for the second time, you go trudging through the trailer.

You find your MawMaw in her recliner, dozing off.

You give her a little shake because she's so deaf that screaming bloody murder won't do a lick of good.

She wakes with a short, pig-like squeal, as if you've shocked her into a heart attack, even though you're the only person with the job of waking her old ass up anymore.

Your MawMaw might have been a pretty woman once. All the photos of her when she was young were burnt up by her second husband, your real, blood-related grandpa. The man you'd called your Pappy had been her third husband before he keeled over dead in that very piss-kitchen. But your real grandpa didn't want your MawMaw thinking she was pretty, even all those years ago. Didn't want her thinking she was anything but his baby-making, church-going, God-fearing Delta wife.

You suppose she must have been pretty enough for there to be a reason to burn them photos. As for yourself, you don't really have much of an idea of what you look like, and you like it that way. All you need to know is that you got two eyes, two eyebrows, a nose, a mouth, and no one shrieks in terror at the sight of you when you go into the Piggly Wiggly for collard greens.

"The hell you want?" says MawMaw, glaring at you with them droopy eyes that make you hope you never get old.

"Weatherman says it's fixin' to snow."

That's enough to get MawMaw up and screaming, hooting like a goose, and flapping her arms like one, too.

And because she's old and weird and scared of catching the cancer bug from snow-prone air—another one of the Reverend's fun facts—she sends you to bring the cows in.

MawMaw's trailer—shit, you guess now it's *your* trailer, too—isn't much to look at, just some metal and peeling paint, but the pasture's pretty nice, as far as pastures go. Though you have to be honest here: pastures don't go very far. And you're not really sure if it even counts as a one, because pastures are probably supposed to have fences. Y'all just let them cows roam free and hope they come home with most of their limbs.

As for outside, it isn't that bad, but there's a weird sort of something in the air. Not snow just yet. Something like *anticipation*—one of Uncle Bubba's favorite words. Your breath comes out solid—moving through the air like creamer in coffee. The cold eats away at your hunting socks and yellow rain boots, making your feet feel like the frozen grapes you and your siblings eat in the summertime when the A.C. goes out. Three sweatshirts aren't enough for this cold, but you got cows to bring in. Plus, MawMaw probably won't let you back in the trailer without them.

"ALL Y'ALL COME ON NOW!" you bellow, stomping your feet and clapping your hands. You've forgotten gloves so your skin stings with each slam of your palms.

You see them cows towards the edge of the pasture, shrugging their heavy bovine shoulders and swishing their tails even though you know they hear you. Your Daddy says you've got the booming voice of a true Delta woman—which is about the nicest thing he's ever said to you.

"DON'T MAKE ME COME OUT THERE!"

They don't.

The cows, the closest things you have to siblings now that you're living with MawMaw, come trotting in. You know the resistance was just for show. They're even colder than you because, they don't have hunting socks on.

You shove their big asses through the little door of the trailer and the living room floorboards creak under their weight. But you know they won't break. Before he died, Pappy reinforced the foundation for this very reason.

Now you've got a living room full of cows and your job is done.

"MawMaw!" you call. "I got 'em in!"

"Then come help me with all this boilin' water!"

You leave the cows on the couch after making them promise not to shit on the nice rug from the Jackson Target. After some attitude, they moo in agreement.

In the piss-kitchen, MawMaw has five pots of water going on the stove and a pile of hot water bottles with skin older than hers on the counter.

"We gotta keep warm, baby," she says when she hears the squeak of your rain boots. It's a familiar sound to her from years ago—these boots used to be your Ma's. "You know what the Reverend says about this snow."

"It's demonic, I know, MawMaw."

"And over my dead body will the Devil get to my grandbaby."

You laugh because that's all you can do when MawMaw gets to talking about good ole Lucifer.

"The Devil don't want me, MawMaw, I promise."

That's when you see it. Outside the single-paned window is the answer to your Uncle Bubba's prayers.

Snow.

You, MawMaw, and the cows sleep in the living room that night, each bundled up in five layers and holding a hot water bottle.

When you wake up that morning, the curtains are open, and the cows are starting to get antsy. You can hear MawMaw in the piss-kitchen, frying eggs and listening to the radio. She's singing along to Elvis and Dolly and grumbling at the ads for interrupting her music. The light coming in from the windows is tinged with hues of blue, nothing like the yellow warmth of summer.

You're at peace, but your toes are freezing, and your hot water bottle is no more than lukewarm.

One of the cows licks your face.

"Eudora!" you exclaim, pushing her away. "If you don't quit that I'll tell God on you!"

Eudora stops. In the South, even cows are God-fearing.

"Baby doll?" MawMaw calls. "You awake?"

"Yeah?"

You should've pretended to be asleep, because now you're outside in the driveway holding a plastic shovel from the one time your family went to the Gulf Coast. "Clear the driveway," MawMaw had said, tossing you the shovel, already cracked in two places. If you'd had any sense, you would have faked a heart attack or just dropped dead right there, but no, you heeded the Reverend's last sermon about honesty. So, now you're freezing to death in the most hodgepodge snow outfit, which is God-awful, even for Mississippi.

The hodgepodge outfit is this: two pairs of hunting socks, yellow rain boots circa 1980, Walmart leggings under your thickest pair of blue jeans, a couple of long sleeve t-shirts, three "Visit Mississippi!" sweatshirts, cheap gloves, and a beanie Pappy wore when he started going bald.

But the snow is beautiful.

You don't use the word beautiful often. People drop it too much, you think. Uncle Bubba used to talk about saying words so much they lost their meaning. You think beautiful is one of those words, so you use it sparingly, only when you really mean it.

Today, as much as your fingers ache with cold, you mean it.

This snow isn't like the Hallmark movies. It's thinner, muddier, and grimy like the Yazoo clay beneath it. It crunches under the yellow rain boots, the sweetest sound you've heard in a while. Icicles hang from the edge of the trailer's roof, and a thin layer of ice coats the dying azalea bushes flanking the front door.

This snow wouldn't be beautiful to most people but, you aren't most people.

Sure, it's out of place here in your subtropical home, but it is an honest attempt at something else.

You tell yourself that this is what Uncle Bubba wanted as you scoop snow out of the gravel driveway, hunched over like that weird guy from Notre Dame. Your head's starting to pound—you're pretty sure you're allergic to the cold. You've got Mississippi blood, and Mississippi blood is quick to freeze.

You're starting to understand snow. It's the freezer aisle in the grocery store after a day spent at the public pool, a brain freeze from a snow cone, and a cold shower when the water heater's out. Snow is all these moments rolled into one.

You're singing some Dolly to yourself when the neighbor boy stumbles over. The stumbling is because one leg is shorter than the other—probably a screw-up on heaven's part.

You don't say anything because this is Ole Colby Jackson, and your MawMaw told you not to talk to Ole Colby Jackson.

"That Jackson boy is the kinda boy to take flowers from girls, if you catch my meaning," she'd said.

You're not quite sure you did catch her meaning, but you keep a close watch on the azalea bushes whenever Ole Colby Jackson is around. And he sure does have a thieving look about him. He's the kind of boy that would have been good-looking if he didn't have the face he was born with. But his biceps are like a cottonmouth snake that had just swallowed a mouse—in other words, real nice. You only notice this because he is wearing a wife-beater, bootcut jeans, and a cowboy hat, as if he doesn't notice the snow on the ground.

As much as a Southern girl you are, Southern boys will never make sense to you.

"Hey, you," he says. You keep your eyes trained on the ground and your posture hunched.

"My MawMaw told me not to talk to you." You keep your voice as flat and well-annunciated as you can—if you give these boys an inch, they take a yard.

He bends down to your level, making him even wonkier than before. "Why not?" And he sounds genuinely hurt.

"She said you take flowers from girls. And I'm a girl."

Ole Colby Jackson slips his hat farther back on his head, revealing a wild crop of blonde hair. You don't trust blondes for plenty of good reasons.

"Well, I ain't never deflowered no one," he says. "You can't exactly do that when you've got all your flowers yourself."

You aren't convinced. His untrustworthy blonde hair reflects the white light coming off the snow.

"Those are MawMaw's azalea bushes, so I best not catch you anywhere near them."

He crinkles up his nose. "You think I'm tryin' to deflower your MawMaw?"

You're starting to get annoyed at this point. "Did I not just say that my MawMaw said that you take flowers from people? Don't be stupid, boy. And you better not take any of my flowers once I plant them come spring!"

He just stares at you for a bit, and you lift your face to meet his flower-stealing gaze.

"Would you just go on and get?" you say with venom unfit for a lady.

There's a moment where no one speaks. A stone of tension forms in your lungs because, looking in his face is just so damn awkward.

Then, Ole Colby Jackson smiles. Your stomach clenches with anger because he's got more teeth than you expected and this close you can see that his skin doesn't have even a single goosebump on it. Meanwhile, you're shaking like a tree in the wind.

"The hell you smilin' about?" you snap. You want to call him an asshole, but MawMaw has a radar for cuss words and those trailer walls are real thin.

He stands up slow and lopsided, then tips his hat.

"I think we're gonna be friends."

You chuck the beach shovel at him.

Winter nights come early, and despite such an extraordinary day, God makes no more exceptions. He leaves you like He always does, and you end your day in the stuffy living room with a herd of cows and MawMaw sipping a Bud Light. Her eyelids flutter and she yawns like a walrus, even though it's only 6 p.m. The cows are starting to fade too, their big brown eyes falling heavy with sleep as they lay curled up on the couch. They've taken your spot but, you're enough of a gentlewoman to leave them be. So, you shamble down the hallway, blanket wrapped around your shoulders, to what used to be Uncle Bubba's study, and is now your room.

Uncle Bubba didn't care much for neatness, a fact evident by the state of his study, even now. It's just as he'd left it, wall to wall with books and maps and all the trinkets he'd found at estate sales. In the center of the tiny room, your cot is carefully arranged to not disturb any of Uncle Bubba's things. You know it's getting weird, that you are sleeping in a shrine, but you can't bear the thought of moving anything. Because in all the collected dust are flakes of Uncle Bubba's skin and pieces of his wavy brown hair. You can't brush off the last little bits of his body left above ground, you just can't.

The only thing you've touched is the Bible he'd left open on the floor. It is a Catholic Bible—even though neither you nor your uncle had ever known a Catholic—and was left flipped to a story you'd never heard before. The Book of Judith.

You'd scoured the pages for some kind of sign. You'd begged Judith, whoever she was, to tell you what she knew. You'd winced at the brutality of her story but kept reading it over and over again, reliving the moment she cut off the general's head. You'd grown to love Judith, grown to appreciate that she'd been the last one to speak to your uncle. You loved her for her meanness and how all the other Christians excluded her from their Bibles, because mean women don't fit into their world. You loved your Uncle Bubba for finding her for you.

All this makes you think of the Reverend and his talk about Deuteronomy 23:1.

So, you flip the thin Bible pages to the spot and read the smudged words there.

No one whose testicles are crushed or whose penis is cut off shall be admitted to the assembly of the Lord.

Huh.

You knew he was talking shit.

JACKSON
SIREN
CALL

You roll into Jackson, Mississippi at six thirty in the morning, long before most of the city is awake, long before you should be awake if it weren't for this goddamn learner's permit test.

I-55 has your MawMaw's heart skipping beats, but you're staring out the passenger window in awe of the city unfolding before you.

Off the interstate is a Cracker Barrel billboard with a murder of crows perched atop it. And beneath that is an abandoned Hooters, the orange trim gone dingy, and the windows covered with boards. It makes you wonder what kind of place this must be if even a Hooters can't make it.

You suppose this wouldn't be much of a city to anyone else but you and your Delta sensibilities. Hell, you were shocked the first time you saw a Walmart Supercenter.

Downtown is what really has your heart in your throat. You have to crane your neck to see the tops of the buildings, upsetting an old hunting injury from when Isaiah had gotten you in the back of the head with a rifle. Above the skyscrapers is the clouds, and above the clouds are the airplanes coming in and out of Medgar Evers Airport. You wonder what it would be like to sit in one of those planes, and whether they feel like you're flying in a tin can hurtling through the air. Mostly, you wonder where you'd go. If you're honest, you've never really thought farther than Mississippi.

But here on the ground, your MawMaw's fixing to hyperventilate. She'd taken an exit she wasn't supposed to, right into the belly of the city. You've got the map laid across your lap with the route from Ass Crack to the Pearl DMV highlighted. But you let her take the exit because Jackson is calling to you. It's the call of a million-year-old smoker, yet you listen, wondering if this is what Willie Joe heard all the way in Ass Crack.

All the hospitals loom over the road, casting shadows over Pappy's old truck. You know that's where they send Delta people when God's about to take them home because a Delta hospital can't do shit to save your life. You remember how the nurses out in Greenville stuck Old Man Quitman's catheter in wrong and he had to be airlifted to Jackson so they could fix it there.

"How in the Devil's underpants do you put a catheter in wrong?" your MawMaw had said. "Lord above, there's only one hole!"

Even though it's early, there are people shambling about the streets. They walk like they're on something. You may be country, but country people know about drug addicts better than anyone. Ass Crack is crawling with them. It's another one of those things no one talks about unless it's to claim your Uncle Bubba overdosed. And you know that's not true, because even though he drank like a fish, your Uncle Bubba was too afraid of needles to ever shoot anything up.

You pass a college with big iron gates. You know it isn't Willie Joe's school—no, hers is deeper in the city. She's gone as far as you can go, and you don't blame her.

The roads are rife with potholes bouncing Pappy's old truck so violently that your head cracks against the window every so often. You swear you see one big enough to take a bath in. That's the first thing any person tells you about Jackson—that the potholes are big enough to swim in.

Your MawMaw is cussing up a storm because the two of you are lost as all hell and now the state capitol is staring y'all in the face.

"It's pretty," you say. You'd been inside once on the elementary school field trip to Jackson. The House of Representatives Chamber had dazzled you with its domed roof and marble columns. Then Ole Colby Jackson had shit himself where the Governor usually sits.

You're trying to see the bright side so, you mumble, "At least we got to see all this."

MawMaw just cusses you out. She's in that kind of mood. You think she might have decided to quit smoking again.

You eventually get to the DMV, passing Whitfield on the way.

Whitfield is another one of those places that Delta folk talk about all the time, though they've likely never been there themselves. And that's because it's what Uncle Bubba would call *infamous*, and MawMaw would call "the crazy house." Sometimes she still uses the old name, Mississippi State Lunatic Asylum, when she's had one too many glasses of gas station wine.

"It sure is crazy that they used to call it that," someone would say.

Then you would all laugh because someone said crazy.

"They've tried to send me down to Whitfield a few times," Uncle Bubba used to joke before the wild coyotes got him. Sometimes you weren't sure if it really was a joke.

"Down to Whitfield," is one of them Mississippi phrases that holds a particularly soft space in your heart. Only Mississippi mouths, tongues, and teeth shape that phrase, making it special, at least to you.

But the Pearl DMV isn't anything special, unless you count the prison across the street. As MawMaw puts Pappy's old truck in park, you stare at the barbed wire fences encasing the prison grounds, wondering what all those people did to end up there.

MawMaw catches you gazing at the gray concrete watch towers and is quick to say, "That's where your ass is fixin' to end up if you keep actin' up in school."

You don't say nothing, just flip through your pirated learner's permit study guide. If you fail this test MawMaw will kill you dead—even if it sends her to the prison or Whitfield—because driving you three hours to Jackson is already eating into her day-drinking time.

"You better know your shit, girl," MawMaw says, then clambers ungracefully out of the truck. She hasn't bent her knees fully in years so it's more of a controlled fall than anything.

You climb out after her, clutching the packet of paper tight enough to absorb the information through your skin. This whole test thing seems a bit silly to you. Even though you've been driving the tractor since you were seven and three quarters, you've got to take a written test to prove you can drive. You don't think that's fair to most of the Delta rednecks you know—the only thing they *can* do is man a combine.

It's seven o'clock and there's already a line at the door. You notice instantly that there isn't a smile in sight.

That's one thing they say about the Pearl DMV: it'll send you either across the street or down the road.

Knowing your MawMaw, both results are more than possible.

In line, she's leaning heavy on her cane, grumbling to herself about city slickers and good-for-nothing government bullshit. You're standing next to her, observing the Jackson people as they fall into the line. They've all got a kind of crazy flash in their eyes. On second glance, it's a hell of a lot like the Delta people you know. You suppose this wildness might just be a Mississippi thing.

But sure as hell, these Jackson people are far more technologically advanced than Delta folks. They've all got flip phones pressed to their ears and iPods in their back pockets.

In front of you is a boy, slightly older, standing by himself. And he sure seems like a character dressed head to toe in camo, even including his Crocs—in leisure mode, of course—and his hair sticks straight up out of his scalp like a porcupine's quills.

There's something a slightly askew about the boy that you can't quite place, so you stare at him for a while. Evidently, he feels your eyes on the back of his head. After a minute of staring, he whips around and looks you right in your face.

His eyes contain that white hot Jackson crazy, burning like lava and muddy like the Pearl River. You hate to admit it, but you feel something akin to fear as his gaze tears into you.

"Hi," he says, voice like a tin roof in the wind. "How y'all doing?"

You know your MawMaw isn't in the mood for this boy, but she's Southern. So, she plasters a smile on her face and says, "Doing about as well as you can at this here DMV. How you doing, sugar?"

Then she whacks you with the palm of her hand and hisses, "The boy asked you a question, girl."

“I’m good,” you croak out.

Now you remember MawMaw talking a bunch of shit last night about presenting yourself nice down in Jackson so all those city slickers don’t think you’re some good-for-nothing Delta trash. You look around at the DMV crowd and wonder if they’re the kind of people whose opinions you ought to care about.

“I’m good myself, except for all my nerves about my driver’s test,” says the boy.

“Oh, you’ll do fine, son. I’m sure you’re quite the driver,” MawMaw says.

The boy laughs. “Nah, I’m a pretty dog shit driver. I’ve failed that test four goddamn times.”

“I didn’t know they let you take it that many times,” you say, and MawMaw smacks the back of your head.

Your ears are ringing, but the boy doesn’t seem offended. He just smiles a wide smile, showing a mouth full of metal, and leans in real close to you. You want to hit him for breathing in your face like this, but MawMaw’s still on her kick about politeness.

“They let you take it as many times as you want when you’re a fugitive like me.”

You scoff. “All right then.”

His eyes flash with that Jackson fire. “I’m serious as gas prices, baby. I’m responsible for most of the potholes in this city. They call me,” he pauses for dramatic effect. “Billy the Pothole Kid.”

You want to call bullshit on Billy the Pothole Kid, but something in you—probably the part related to Uncle Bubba—tells you this wild talking boy isn't telling you a lie.

"What'd you do all that for?" you ask.

Billy the Pothole Kid shrugs and flashes his braces at you again. "I've just been feeling like I've gotta make some holes in the road."

You grunt in response.

He cracks his neck. "And lately, I've been feeling like I gotta make some holes in other places, too."

When they finally open the doors, a wave of misery tumbles out, making your eyes water. MawMaw doesn't seem to be affected. She grabs you by the arm and drags you inside, cutting more than a few people in line, though Billy the Pothole Kid stays firmly in front of y'all. All the folks MawMaw cuts open their mouths to fight her, but she raises her cane, and they pipe down real quick.

A few years ago, you would have been mortified, but she does this kind of thing in McDonald's when the line's too long and she's really hankering for a Quarter Pounder. Living with MawMaw has given you a tolerance for embarrassment matched only by drunks and stand-up comedians.

You get up to the front faster than a jackrabbit on cocaine, thanks to MawMaw's lack of decorum. The lady working the table looks so ancient you worry that she might kick the bucket mid-sentence. She gives the two of you a long, drawn-out glare, but says nothing about the cutting. You suppose she doesn't get paid enough to deal with all that.

You smile at her. She rolls her eyes.

"We need to get this young'un a learner's permit," declares your MawMaw.

The lady says nothing, just hands you a shit ton of forms and rasps, "Your number is D45. Now go sit down."

For once in her life, MawMaw follows an order, and y'all find two empty seats next to the vending machine solely stocked with pork rinds. MawMaw fills out the forms with a pen she stole from the church pew and hollers your social security number to the whole damn building. You swear you spot Billy the Pothole Kid scribbling it down.

As for the building itself, dust seem to cover every surface, even the patrons. The old man in the seat next to you chews dip loudly, smacking his lips together like a cow. In the seat next to him is a roach enjoying a lint-covered potato chip.

Roaches don't bother you too much. You had to learn to coexist with them at a young age after Daddy lost his job in the Recession and y'all couldn't pay for the exterminator no more. They used to scurry in the walls of that old house, chattering so loud they kept you up for days. Colton and Isaiah had the job of killing them with rolled-up newspapers and Daddy's shotgun. You'll never forget the roach that didn't die even after Colton fired an entire round into its exoskeleton. They always say that Mississippi bugs are something else. That was the moment you knew they were right.

The old man slips the roach a tiny bit of dip. You aren't all that surprised when it starts to chew, waving its antenna from the nicotine buzz. You'd ask for some yourself, but your Uncle Bubba used to chew dip and he had barely any teeth by the time he dropped dead.

The woman across from you hollers at the sight of the roach. Both the old man and the roach give her a dirty look. She shuts up.

You're starting to understand why the DMV would send someone to Whitfield. The lights are somehow too faint and too bright all at the same time. The air has a foggy quality to it and the lingering scent of cigarette smoke. The tiles are checkered a dingy green and cream, a color that reminds you of Isaiah's vomit after MawMaw's spinach dip went bad at the family reunion.

All of that considered, the air of the place is *off*. Something in this building is wrong and everyone knows it. Still, it seems the Mississippi government is too cheap to care.

A few ages and dip cans later, D43 is called, and Billy the Pothole Kid stands up. He makes his way up to the counter with an oddly graceful gait, almost like he's floating over the slum of the DMV.

When she sees him, the lady at the counter sighs. "Well, here you are again, William. Maybe the fifth time's the charm."

Billy the Pothole Kid grins his metal-filled grin. "I think today's my day, Miss Charlene."

She sighs. "I hope so. Your instructor's gonna be out front in a bit."

He blows Miss Charlene a kiss on his way out, confident as ever. You wonder if Crocs are good driving shoes.

You're only two numbers away from the test, and your heartbeat is starting to pick up. The packet is damp with the sweat from your palms. You can sense MawMaw giving you the eye, probably saying a spiteful prayer to the Lord for your success. Most of her prayers are tinged with ill will, something that never seemed very Christlike to you.

You're in the midst of reviewing the meaning of road signs when you hear a deafening roar. The building quakes around you, accompanied by screams of terror. You throw your arms over your head, vaguely remembering the tornado drills at school.

Your MawMaw topples out of her chair, cane clattering to the ground. She shrieks, "Oh Lord! It's the rapture!"

"It's gone hot!" hollers the old man beside her. "Russia dropped the nukes!"

Even in your panic, you have half a mind to wonder if the Cold War hadn't ended years ago.

"God spare me!" your MawMaw cries, clutching her two bad knees.

Through the ruckus around you, you hear the dip-chewing cockroach fly off with a quick buzz. You think, *them roaches are gonna outlive all of us two-legged fools*.

As suddenly as the noise arrived, it ceases. The DMV falls under the blanket of silence. Hesitantly, you pick your head up and meet the gaze of Billy the Pothole Kid.

He's standing amongst the wreckage of a red Volkswagen Jetta, grinning that madman grin. You can't figure out how he got the thing in here. Then you notice the gaping hole behind his imposing camo figure. It reveals the gray winter sky, a fitting back drop for such a criminal as him. Cheap bricks and dry wall surround the wrecked car as it smokes and sputters. Its hood is folded like origami crane. You see the driving test administrator huddled in the passenger seat, seemingly unharmed but certainly scared shitless.

All you can say is, "What in the fresh hell?"

Billy the Pothole Kid's smile never falters. You've got trauma-induced tunnel vision—an Uncle Bubba vocabulary word—and the glint of his braces is all you can see in the madness of the destroyed DMV. You almost want to ask why he's done such a thing, but you remember the many lectures about strange men, especially strange Jackson men.

Miss Charlene pops up from under her desk, fuming mad. "William!" she screams with her megaphone voice. "I'll make you wish you were never born, son!"

She starts climbing over the desk and Billy the Pothole Kid, knowing this is no empty threat, darts out the hole he just made in the wall. Just before he goes, he flashes you a wink.

Big city living sure is something.

MawMaw makes you wait the five hours it takes for them to get the DMV up and running because "I drove three hours down here and I sure ain't making that godforsaken drive again." You choose not to argue. It's easier that way.

The test is simpler than you expected. MawMaw was making it sound like only the smartest kids in Mississippi ever managed to get a license. "Now our Colton really struggled with this test," she'd said on the drive down. "Don't go in there expecting to ace the damn thing, but also know you ain't got an option not to, or I'll whoop your ass right there in that DMV."

You pass in less than five minutes.

When you walk out of the room and give MawMaw a thumbs up, she smiles. She actually smiles. You feel a small blossom of pride in your chest, warm like melted butter.

You walk to Miss Charlene's desk, your head held high. "I passed," you say.

"Congratulations, honey," she says absentmindedly, drywall flakes still in her hair. "Now go down there and take the eye test then you're good to go."

Your right eye is perfect. You read the letters out in your clearest, least Southern voice.

But your left eye. Oh shit, your left eye.

"There's nothing there," you say in disbelief as you stare through the lens at the white screen. You look up at Miss Charlene, right eye still closed. "Ma'am, I think your test is broken."

Miss Charlene's expression is one of pity.

"Oh baby," she says. "I think it's your eye that's broken."

Needless to say, you fail the eye test.

Telling MawMaw goes about as well as you'd expect. She hollers, she cusses, she tells Miss Charlene to give you the permit anyway, then turns on you, shouting nearly indecipherable words. She's gone so Southern even you can't comprehend most of it. You gather that she's angry about your "useless" left eye and your "useless" self in general.

As she herds you out of the DMV, still cussing up a storm, you can't help but remember that she never thought your third cousin Willie Joe to be all that useful. And isn't she the one who made it all the way to Jackson?

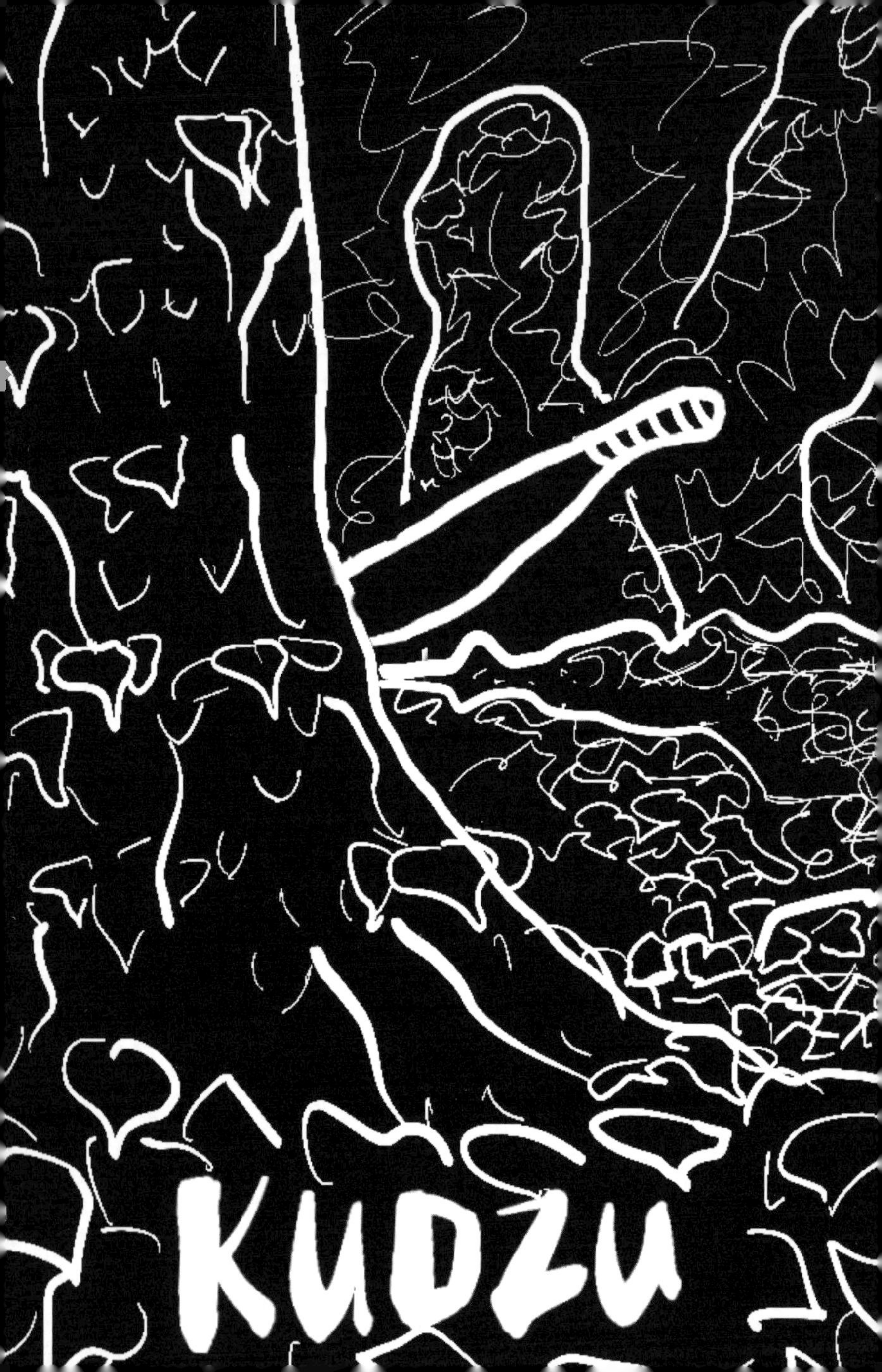
KUDZU

DETENTION

When it hits three o'clock and the bell rings, you don't get to go home. That's because you've got detention for asking too many questions in Bible class again. Which means you're outside the school hacking at kudzu with a machete that your English teacher lent you. You don't get the point of fighting the kudzu, because it's been winning this battle ever since some fool brought it over from Japan and made it all of the South's problem. That's the real psychological torture of this kind of detention: fighting a battle that can't be won.

The sun beats down on you, cooking your skin through one of your Daddy's old t-shirts. It's hot out, because it always is, but at least it hasn't hit a hundred today. When the English teacher gave you the machete, she told you to be careful because there's a heat advisory. Giant blade in hand, you told the Reverend this, but he only told you, "the heat will burn the sin out of you, child." You wanted to ask him if that's why Hell is hot, but, for once, you decided against running your mouth.

So now you're swinging the machete like a wild woman, taking down swaths of kudzu with each cut. The vines fall around you like innards, reminding you of the violent computer games Isaiah plays behind your Ma's back. He used to wait until midnight to sneak down to the ancient desktop y'all kept in the family room. Sometimes you'd follow him and watch him shoot people in the head with one click of the mouse. When he pissed you off, you'd want to tell on him, but you knew part of siblinghood is keeping secrets. Isaiah didn't tell Ma when he caught you reading *Harry Potter and the Sorcerer's Stone* out in the barn—she'd banned it over the whole witchcraft thing. The two of you were stuck in a stalemate, much like the push and pull between you and the kudzu you're desperately trying to vanquish.

With every fall of the machete, you let out a cuss word you know the Reverend wouldn't approve of. He might have the power to give you detention over one too many questions about Leviticus, but at least you can mutter "fuck" under your breath when he isn't around. Like Uncle Bubba used to say, *it's the little things*.

The kudzu isn't little. No, there's an entire sea of it out behind the school, covering telephone poles and pine trees in a leafy green cage. It makes you feel like a needle in a haystack, skinny and itchy.

Sweat beads in your armpits and runs down your sides, leaving you damp and miserable and Mississippian to your core. Your hair is plastered to your forehead, the kind of unruly that your MawMaw would shudder at.

That's when Ole Colby Jackson comes trudging up, much to your irritation. He's sweating like a pig, and by that you mean not at all. Fun fact: pigs don't sweat. Of course, he's wearing that damn wife beater and blue jeans, but instead of a cowboy hat he's pulled a baseball cap over his wild crop of blond hair.

You make a sound you can only describe as pure hatred because you really do hate that boy something fierce. Even if he's one of the only people who's ever bothered with you.

"Go away," you grunt, deciding on a more direct approach this time.

Since Ole Colby Jackson is dumber than a pile of rocks, he doesn't seem to get it.

"Doin' all right, neighbor?" he asks, flashing you that classic Delta boy grin that your Ma always told you to watch out for.

"Them Delta boys'll charm you right into the sack, but you can't let 'em. You hear me girl?" she'd said.

You still don't understand exactly what potato sack racing has to do with any of it, but you suppose your Ma would know better than you.

And Ole Colby Jackson is still standing there flashing his oddly clean teeth.

"Haven't you heard, fool?" you say in between slashes of the machete.

Ole Colby Jackson seems confused by that, but, in fairness, he seems confused by everything.

"Heard what?"

"Heard that I'm not supposed to be talking to you!" you exclaim, bringing the blade down hard on a particularly stubborn vine.

"Why not?"

You decide not to answer. You take your anger out on the kudzu, knowing full well it will all be back tomorrow before first period.

"What'd you do?" asks Ole Colby Jackson.

"What?"

"I mean, you only get kudzu detention if you do something really bad...so, what did you do?"

You shrug. It's not that you're ashamed of all you've done, it's more that you're already out of breath from hacking at vines.

"You mouth off to the Reverend again?" says Ole Colby Jackson, raising one eyebrow. That slight movement of his face makes you hate him even more because you really wish you could do that. Such an expression would add so much to your performance in the church Christmas play. Maybe they'd even let you be a wise man instead of the camel.

"I don't mouth off," you say. "I just ask questions and he gets his underpants in a twist over them."

Ole Colby Jackson cracks a smile. "What you doin' thinkin' about the Reverend's underwear?"

"You really wanna try and piss me off while I'm holding a machete?"

Ole Colby Jackson makes the only intelligent decision you've ever seen him make. He changes the subject.

"You know what you need?" he says.

"What?"

"Some goats up in this bitch."

You give him a look and he opens his mouth to explain, but you walk off before he can. You have no desire to listen to his bullshit. You're already well aware goats eat kudzu, and you're also in desperate need of water. The English teacher was right about that heat advisory. The afternoon sun is tough on even the most hardened Delta people like yourself.

You stroll through the school hallway, machete dangling loosely in your grip. The air-conditioning, shitty as it is, washes over you like milk and honey. The lukewarm water from the drinking fountain tastes better than fried chicken after church. You barely even notice the couple a few feet away devouring each other's faces.

After a moment, you realize that it's Tallulah who has the starting quarterback pressed up against the lockers.

You suppose this is why the Reverend's always glaring at her during his lectures. The Bible specifically warns against face-sucking in the school hallway.

You're thinking it would be best to wait a bit before you head back outside to kudzu and that damn Jackson boy. So, you go wandering through the school, eyeing the photographs on the wall that catalogue the few awards students have won. You spy your third cousin Willie Joe real quick, since she was the only one in her year doing anything but drinking in the Walmart parking lot. No, she was winning poetry awards left and right and shocking all of Ass Crack. Your Uncle Bubba used to say she was the only one in the family with a literary bone in her body.

You eye her photograph for a while, taking in her big eyes and reluctant smile. Those eyes are a lot like your Ma's—big, brown, and a little worn out. She doesn't look much like you aside from the way her hair sticks up in the back. That cowlick makes you wonder about your own literary bones.

The winning poem is framed on the wall next to her photo, printed on light blue cardstock in Times New Roman point 12, which is about as money the school would shell out for non-sports achievements.

"Dirt Mother Running"

Backside to balcony,
Window woman take me in, take him home,
Thrumming fingers ask to cry
And to howl deep in my bones.
So, love is all and always,
Wouldn't it be sweet to find something else?

I'd go home if I could live that way,
I'd find the hours and count the days
Away from it.
And dig.
And dig.
Find concrete bones.

Shout out a song for this one beer body.

Something in that poem makes your mouth hurt. You typically feel all your emotions in your teeth. The dentist calls it a cavity, but you call it feelings.

Willie Joe's poem makes you want to tug your molars right out your head and holler. The Reverend wishes he would string words together like that—*I'd go home if I could live that way*—easy and heart wrenching and full of tooth-aching feeling. God is surely speaking through your third cousin, and you're starting to doubt whether the Reverend knows Him at all.

The machete starts to feel heavy in your hand and suddenly you're hot again. Your sweat glands pick up again, galloping like wild horses.

You think this heat is Uncle Bubba. He finally found his way to you and, dear God, you've got the puking feeling in your throat again—all because you can't help but think about him in a car accident, in those trees, drowning, falling off the roof, or another one of the ways your MawMaw rationalizes his death. In her mind, he's dead and it don't matter how.

But your Uncle Bubba would want the truth.

And he'd want you of all people to understand it.

No. Not today.

But you know at least one truth. It would be disrespectful to throw up in front of a family member's poem, especially such a beautiful one. So, you choke it down like a good Southern Baptist girl.

The vomit is acid in your throat and probably about to burn a hole through your esophagus, leaving you like your great uncle who smoked too much. Every time you blink, you see Willie Joe's words behind your eyelids. *Wouldn't it be sweet to find something else?*

It's holding you hostage in your own mind, this goddamn poem. All that's built up is trying to get out somehow, whether it be through tears or puke.

But the school isn't for escaping feelings. Plus, you can hear the couple down the hall getting closer, sliding against the lockers with a drawn-out metallic rustle. On occasion, you hear a bang. That Tallulah has a dominating way about her.

To free yourself from the clutches of the school, you have to walk past the couple again. You try to ignore the coyote-like sounds they're making and keep your eyes trained straight forward. Although you don't really feel like you're intruding at all, because they're the ones going at it in the school hallway and Tallulah would tell you everything about that boy's mouth if you'd let her.

Outside, the heat is just as intense as before, turning your stomach like a washing machine. Even so, that's well within the range of normal. The goat, however, is not.

It's standing completely still before the kudzu forest, looking at you with its dark eyes. Around its neck is a tag. You can just barely see something scrawled on it.

Since you've never been particularly afraid of goats, you march towards it, waving the machete and hollering like a cave person. The goat doesn't move, just keeps blinking at you. You get the sense that it knows something. There's a military air about this creature and you quickly realize it's not budging. Once you're close enough to smell the clover stuck in its fur, you snatch the card from its neck. The scrawl reads, *This is Judith. She's here to help. From: Colby Jackson.*

That damn Colby Jackson.

You look at Judith. Judith looks at you.

"Well?" you say.

She refuses to be ruffled by your forceful tone. She simply trots towards the kudzu forest, delicately stepping over the vines you've already hacked. Then she lets out a small, sharp bleat. And the kudzu comes crawling off the trees.

You stare as vines move like snakes down the trunks, rustling quietly. They settle at Judith's feet, as if they were offerings to some pagan god resting atop an altar. For the first time in your life, you're seeing what lies under the sea of kudzu—dead pines stripped of branches and needles rotten from lack of sun.

The machete hits the ground with a thud. Judith looks at you, almost smugly. She lets out another little bleat and, somehow, you understand her.

"Sometimes you just have to ask nicely," she says.

Kudzu Dentention

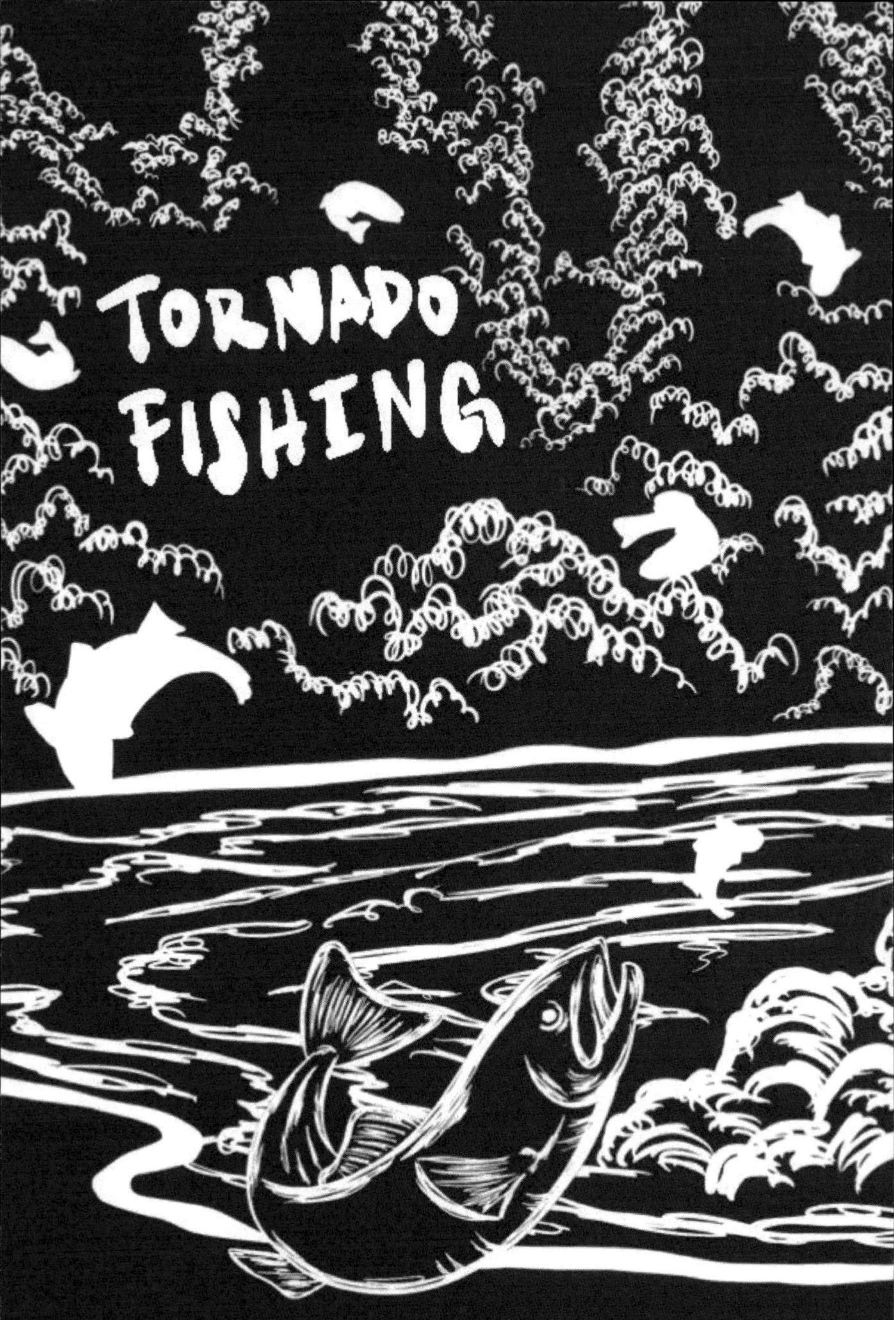
TORNADO
FISHING

When tornadoes come, it isn't nothing special until the moment someone dies. But ever since one ripped the roof off the school with all the kids cowering in the halls, they've started sending y'all home every time anyone even hears the word tornado—not that you're complaining. And after the last inspection of the new-ish roof, the school board decided that it would actually be safer to stand out in the middle of a field than be in that school during a tornado. You suppose that makes sense. The gym does have quite a few holes in the ceiling.

The principal comes over the intercom while you're in math class pretending to find the hypotenuse.

"My granny up in Rosedale gave me a call and said that they're fixin' to get a tornader and that the wind man on the television said it might come rip us a new one down here. Y'all know the drill. Get the Hell outta here."

A cheer arises from the math class. Even your teacher looks relieved to be rid of you hellions. Tallulah, who's taken to sitting in front of you ever since she called you "punk rock," whips around to you and says, "sure is a good thing I wore my *tornader eyeliner* today."

You're not exactly sure what constitutes *tornader eyeliner*, but you suppose it's that smudgy look Tallulah likes to go for. You think it suits her silt irises.

"You look like a raccoon," you tell Tallulah as the two of you shove your things into your backpacks.

"Thanks, bitch," she says.

Your heart skips a beat, and you feel your face twist into a look of confusion. You've been called a bitch before, but never with the tone Tallulah is using. You suppose it's another one of her isms that you just don't understand.

She walks out of the room with you, chatting away about some boy from Delta State she met at a bar she wasn't supposed to be at. She's started doing that recently, following you places. She waits for you at your locker after class and sits across from you at lunch. You want to tell her that she's cutting into your reading time, but your MawMaw's lectures about politeness always pop into your head before you open your mouth.

At your locker now, and Tallulah has moved onto talking about how the toilet wine sales have gone down ever since their number one provider went back to prison. Most of your responses are just grunts. She doesn't seem to care.

As you rifle through your stacks of contraband novels, she leans against the metal lockers and lights a cigarette. She's one of the few people bold enough to smoke indoors. When it comes to tobacco, the Reverend's like a bloodhound.

"Some folks smoke in a redneck way," she'd said once. "I smoke in a *French* way."

You don't particularly see the difference. You suppose you just aren't European enough.

Now you're trying to decide which novel to take home for some storm shelter reading, something Maw-Maw wouldn't bat an eye at. Finding such a book is proving quite the feat.

"Why're you always reading?" Tallulah blurts between puffs of cigarette smoke. She was always asking you questions like that.

"'Cause I wanna," you say, turning your attention back to deciding between *The Optimist's Daughter* and *Delta Wedding*.

"But why do you wanna whenever no one else ever does?" Tallulah presses.

You consider that for a moment.

"Because the Reverend has banned most of the things I read."

Tallulah's eyes light up. "That's fucking metal."

There was another one of her phrases you don't get.

"No, it's paper," you say.

Then she laughs like you've said something funny.

"Well, I gotta scoot," she says, stomping her cigarette butt on the floor. "The fourth best looking guy on the basketball team offered to drive me home today."

Then she winks. Tallulah usually winks when she talks about boys.

"Then scoot," you say with a quick wave of your hand.

"See you tomorrow." And she starts down the hall, strutting like a darker haired Dolly Parton.

You turn back to your books. As the tornado siren starts to wail, you finally decide. *Delta Wedding* it is.

Back at MawMaw's trailer, you're home herding the cattle into the living room. The cows aren't giving you their usual attitude, probably because they can sense the danger in the air. Plus, the sky's gone a bit green. Still, they stink to high heaven from all the rain and surely, you'll smell like wet cow come tomorrow no matter how many times you hose off out back.

"MawMaw!" you start to holler before you remember that MawMaw isn't here. She'd gone to your down-the-street neighbors to hunker down in their cellar and left you to bring in the cows. Typical.

There's a bad feeling settling in your lungs like cigarette smoke, or mustard gas, or whatever they used in the trenches. You've been feeling like this a lot recently, ever since the days got long again and you couldn't sleep through the worst of it. You start wondering if you can bear another Mississippi summer.

A crash of thunder rattles the trailer, and the cows start mooing up a storm.

"Y'all!" you shriek. "It's just thunder, goddamnit!"

One of the cows, mad with terror and weather anxiety, rams into your MawMaw's favorite side table.

"Faulkner, no!" you exclaim, throwing your arms around her neck.

You should have expected this—Faulkner's been skittish ever since the combine nearly got her.

With your fingers tangled around strands of her hair, you try to whisper soothing comforts into the Faulkner's ear. For some reason, "Big Green Tractor" by Jason Aldean is the first thing that comes to mind.

Just when you get the herd to calm down, there's a knock on the door, so loud it ricochets like a bullet through the trailer and startles the cows again. Only one person in the world knocks like that.

You push your way past fear-crazed cows and fling open the front door without even checking the peep hole.

"Isaiah, for Christ's sake!" you holler.

And yeah, it's your second oldest half-brother standing there before you, eyes wild like mad cow disease. You open your mouth to scold him, but he starts talking before you can get a word in.

"Come fishing with me," he urges.

"There's a tornader coming," you say, surprised he managed to miss that.

"Well, that's the best time," Isaiah responds as if it's the most obvious thing in the goddamn world.

Isaiah's never been danger prone. No, he's danger seeking, always sticking his nose in crawfish holes and talking to the county meth head, Mostly Naked John James. The ladies at church can't stand Isaiah because he's always setting fires during service or climbing the sloped roof of the steeple. In his defense, he only burns old hymn books nobody uses anymore, and besides, a little pew fire never hurt no one.

"You wanna come in?" you ask.

Isaiah shakes his head, spraying you with water in the process. It's started raining harder now and the green color of the sky has shifted to something close to purple. You don't really want to keep asking questions. With Isaiah it's usually better not to.

"Come fishing with me," he repeats, elbowing you in the shoulder.

"I have stuff to do," you say sternly.

"No, you don't."

"Yes, I do," you insist. "I've got a book to read and cows to herd."

"But tornader fishin' is real special," says Isaiah. "It only happens as often as it happens, which isn't all that often. So, you oughtacome with."

You think about MawMaw down in the neighbor's cellar without you, probably not even waiting for you to climb down there.

"I'll go if you promise to stop terrorizing the cows with that damn combine," you say.

Isaiah laughs sharp and high, and the cows start behind you. Some of them moo anxiously, as if to warn each other of his presence.

"Fine, you got a deal, sister," he says. "Let's go then!"

You grab the faded rain jacket off the hook by the door and slip your feet into your yellow rain boots. Isaiah's already back in the downpour with only a wild brimmed fishing hat and his gym clothes to protect him.

You make the cows promise to behave, then you lock the door and follow your half-brother outside.

When you step onto the gravel driveway, you notice something.

"Isaiah, where in God's name is the car?"

"There ain't one," Isaiah hollers over the wind. "I biked."

You let out a deeply exasperated sigh.

"Do you even have bait?"

He fishes in his pocket and pulls out a plastic bag filled with wriggling worms.

The whole thing is stupider than anything even Colby Jackson could come up with, and you make sure to tell Isaiah that as he peddles through the rainstorm with you perched on his handlebars to block the rain. He makes you hang onto a huge washbasin which you hold over your head to shield you from the torrential downpour. You feel the worms you shoved in your own pocket squirming against your stomach, probably cursing the day they were born in Ass Crack soil. The racket of the rain hitting the washbasin is deafening, and your clothes are so soaked you might as well be swimming in the Mississippi river.

Tornader fishing, you think to yourself. *Tornader fishing my ass!*

It seems that you're perched on that bike forever, your fingers growing sore and cold from gripping the metal frame.

"Isaiah!" you holler, lifting the basin just slightly and getting a mouthful of rain. "Where the hell—" You have to stop to spit out some water. "—are we going?"

Isaiah shouts something back but you don't hear him over the roar of the tree-breaking wind. This is the problem with brothers, and boys in general. They always get you into some bullshit.

Then, finally, that godforsaken bicycle comes to a stop somewhere you've never been before. Through the rain you see a rusted chain link fence taller than you, even if you were sat on Colton's shoulders. The grass is curling up the metal posts, overgrown and wily like your Daddy's hair used to before he started going bald on the top. The sky has turned an even more menacing shade of purple, but Isaiah doesn't seem to notice, and if he does, he doesn't give a rat's ass. He nudges you off the bike, then hops off himself and tosses it to the ground. Flashing you his signature mischievous smile, he tightens the string of his fishing hat and says, "Let's go."

He starts off walking along the fence and you follow, wishing you'd just stayed with the cows and *Delta Wedding*. Soon, you come across a hole at the bottom of the fence large enough for both of you to squeeze through. Wordlessly, Isaiah does just that, not even stopping when a loose piece of wire catches his shirt. You come through after him, muddying your bare knees as the fence snags stray hairs from your ponytail.

"Why the hell are we doing this?" you snap, wanting to cuss him out.

"Because this is the best fishing spot in the whole damn county," he answers. "Used to be a lumber plant but the state had it walled off some years ago. Some talk about chemicals and shit."

That's when you come across a pond surrounded by another chain link fence. Even through the haze of the rain you can see multiple biohazard signs posted, bright yellow and black like a venomous snake.

Your half-brother is already tossing the washbasin over the fence then climbing after it. He pauses at the top, carefree and confident even with his mouse brown hair plastered to his face.

"What about those signs?" you holler up, anxiety in your voice. You can't help but think about the cancer statistics Uncle Bubba used to rattle off during his rants about the free market and some guy's hand.

"A little biohazard never hurt anybody."

You're about to protest that yes, a little biohazard has hurt anybody, but Isaiah is already over the fence and strolling casually through the pouring rain toward the pond. For a moment you consider turning around and taking the bike back home. The thing is, you haven't a clue where you are. Plus, if you left, what would you ever do with all these worms?

"Fucking tornader fishing," you mutter to yourself and begin your ascent up the fence. You've never been particularly coordinated. No, you didn't get whatever strange form of gracefulness both Isaiah and Colton possess—that must have come from the Reverend. Yet, you make it over the fence through sheer force of will and land right on your tailbone.

The wind has picked up into something fierce. Isaiah stands strong against the storm, never tilting, though his clothes and hat are completely soaked through. The pond churns and splashes like the public pool after the biggest boy in Ass Crack does a cannonball.

"How are we supposed to fish in that?" you holler.

"Just wait, sister," Isaiah says, and plops down right next to the raging pond.

You have no choice but to sit down, too. You pull the bag worms out of your pocket and give them a poke. You're wondering why you do these things, why you go out of your way for these brothers that are only half yours. As you sit there in the mud, something your Uncle Bubba used to say rings in your ears, *the blood of the covenant is thicker than the water of the womb.* You suppose he was right. Shit, it's all about choice. And you chose Colton and Isaiah. The Reverend never did.

Isaiah calls you sister, never indicating halves.

You examine him for a moment, squinting against the raging storm. His mouth is sharp and wide, the nose above it short and mean. All the Reverend, right down to the hellfire eyes.

Sometimes you wonder how Isaiah lives with someone else's face. You've heard the things the ladies in church whisper when they know you're within earshot. *Bastard*, they call him, *but a spitting image of the Reverend*, as if that makes anything better.

Isaiah looks nothing like you, your Ma, or even Colton. Still, there's a covenant of blood between y'all that bridges the gap left by biology.

Why do you bother with halves?

Your brother lays down in the mud and pulls his fishing hat over his face, leaving only his mouth exposed.

"You've been hanging out with that Tallulah girl at school, haven't you?" he says, raindrops collecting in the corners of his mouth.

You shrug. "I mean, she follows me around and talks about herself."

Isaiah laughs. "She's tryin' to be your friend."

"Oh," you say, a lot of things suddenly making sense.

"Does she ever ask about me?"

You scrunch up your nose, suddenly protective of this girl you've finally realized is your friend. "Why do you care if she does?"

Isaiah shrugs. "I just like to know if girls are talking about me."

"Well, she asked about Colton a ton once she realized that he's my older brother."

"Chicks are way too damn into Colton," Isaiah laments. "It's 'cause he's blond and he pulls that Southern gentleman bullshit. And he hasn't even been real blond since he was a kid, for fuck's sake."

"It is more of a dishwater blond," you say.

"Exactly!" Isaiah says, throwing his hands up.

"At least you're smarter than him," you try.

"Girls don't care about smart."

"Yes, they do. Girls have standards, too, you know."

Isaiah grunts in response. Probably because he knows you're right and he doesn't like to tell you that.

"I'm gonna open a gas station after I graduate," he says. "I'll call it Zayah's 24-Hour Jukebox Truck Stop."

"Why 'Zayah's' and not Isaiah's? And are you gonna have a jukebox?"

Isaiah sighs, raising his pointer finger. "Number one. It sounds cooler. Number two. Mind your business."

You suppose that's a good enough answer.

"And how about that Jackson boy?" he taunts.

You scowl instinctively. "What's he got to do with anything?"

"Well, he's a boy that's been hanging around you a bunch and I'm your big brother."

"And what's that supposed to mean?"

Isaiah shrugs, his mouth forming a tight line. "I just don't want you ending up like our Ma." Your silence prompts him to continue. "You know, havin' babies too young."

"Oh." You don't quite see the connection between Colby Jackson and babies, but you'd rather the subject drop since Isaiah's acting weird about it and Isaiah acts weird about nothing.

"It's lucky your Daddy married her," he says. "Saved us all a hell of a lot of trouble."

That's something you do understand. If your Daddy hadn't proposed, she would have become the type of woman they stoned in the Bible.

The wind has picked up so much that there's no use in talking—nothing can be heard over the roar. Yet, Isaiah still has you waiting on the bank of that shitty little pond surrounded by biohazard signs. The worms are growing just as impatient as you are, wriggling around with boredom rather than fear.

You're starting to consider walking home when it finally happens. Just across the pond is the tornado that all of Ass Crack has been screaming about since this morning.

It's just a little thing really, probably only a few feet wide. The one that tore up the town last spring was at least three times as big. Still, this thing is only a football field away and strong enough to rip you in pieces.

Within the swirling mass, you see branches from pine trees and what looks like a few chickens.

"Isaiah!" you scream, even though you know he can't hear you.

He's standing up now, fishing hat whipping in the wind. Your brother, with his preacher's mouth and dangerous way of being, doesn't move one inch in the face of that tornado. In his hands is the silver washbasin. He has a slight smile on his face, that crazy Delta smile you'll never really get used to.

You scream when the tornado hits the pond, throwing water and fish and mud every which way. You press your face into the ground and tangle your fingers in the grass—as if that could stop such a force of nature. You find yourself thinking of your Ma. How she made you let go before you were ready, and packed all your things up while they were putting your Uncle Bubba in the ground. How you're legitimate but the first to go. Because she doesn't really like you, no matter how much she loves you.

The tornado could suck you into the sky at any moment. You don't understand how Isaiah isn't scared. MawMaw always said there was something wrong with him. Something that came from the Reverend.

Then the fish come raining down and you're tossed onto your back, forced to stare at all their writhing bodies dropping from the sky. Their scales are brilliant colors—orange, pink, and blue—against the green of the sky and the dark water crashing around you.

Your uncle is a fish.

You might be joining him soon. That doesn't sound too bad.

And Isaiah is still standing, holding that washbasin out and catching the shining fish like it's nothing. But it is something, and you're almost terrified of him in that moment. He's as sturdy as a Civil War oak with bullets in its trunk, unshaken and unmoved by all that Mississippi has to offer.

Isaiah stands over you now, as you cough up water and start to think up all of the ways you can get him back.

"You good?" he asks. You're unable to answer, half convinced that you're drowning on solid ground.

In his hands is the basin of fish and on his face is that psychotic grin he gets from the Reverend. The worms have managed to escape their prison and are wriggling inside your rain jacket, burrowing into your skin as if you were the earth.

"We caught a shit ton of fish," Isaiah says.

"What?" Another wave of water rushes from your mouth. You look up and make out the shape of a tornado whirling off in the distance. "What the fuck was that?"

"Tornader fishing," he says like it's the most obvious thing in the world.

THE MONEY

This is a reminder to unclench your fists.

You're stiff as a board outside of the school gym, wearing a dress from your MawMaw's hoarding shed out behind her trailer. It's too big, so it falls past your knees and fits you like them dusty old choir robes. MawMaw's friend, Miss Gladys the spinster, had pinned your hair up into something resembling a bird's nest full of loops and loose strands hanging around your ears. Dangling from your neck is a piece of garish costume jewelry your MawMaw picked up from Walmart on the way to the school. Only the shoes are yours—your good church heels, black and practical with a strap around the ankle.

It's the spring formal. You had to go, even though you had a sense you'd end up out here soon enough.

You're alone aside from the boy out for a smoke break. In his creased khaki pants and good cowboy boots, he nurses one of the cheapest cigarettes money can buy. The smoke wafts over to you, and if not for the unholy amount of hairspray keeping the nest intact, your hair would have smelled like smoke for days. Plus, cigarette smoke makes your joints achy, an odd quirk you picked up from your Ma.

Even outside, the bass from the music rattles your teeth and sends your brain jumping around your skull.

It's the typical school dance kind of music, made for dirty dancing and fist pumping.

Every year before the dance, the Reverend calls the whole school into that very gym and gives a long-winded sermon about the dangers of dancing and its Satanic roots.

"Dancing is a gateway to other amoral activities," he's said. "Such as sins of the flesh, blasphemy, simony, fornication, gluttony, hip rotation, and many, many more."

Then he'd grabbed one of the students—the girl who sits in the front of illegal Bible class taking diligent notes—and demonstrated inappropriate dancing. You'd closed your eyes in horror, but no one else had seemed remotely phased by the Reverend thrusting his pelvis into the girl's bottom. You suppose you just aren't holy enough to understand.

It's not like the talk ever does any good. Inside the gym is a pulsating mass of bodies with absolutely no room for Jesus, even if he went on a diet like your Ma. The DJ is just the student body president with a worn-out stereo and an assortment of pirated music. You suppose that's about as good as the dance committee could do with a thirty-dollar budget.

You fiddle with the costume jewelry, attempting to ignore the ache in your fingers and toes. You check your watch. Nine fifteen. You're surprised you held out this long. Last year, Uncle Bubba picked you up at eight forty-five.

You clomp past the cigarette boy, keeping your eyes forward like your MawMaw always says to when you walk past men. In reality, he couldn't care less about you. He doesn't even lift his eyes when you go ungracefully by. You know you're not the prettiest sight with your wasp nest hair and frumpy waistline. Your church shoes pinch your toes and beneath the dress you're sweating like Isaiah after football practice.

You know Isaiah's somewhere in the crowd of ungodly gyration with the girl he took to Hardee's before the dance. You try not to think about what the two of them must be doing, but you have a feeling it's something that would put MawMaw in her grave if she could see it. You'd thought about convincing him to take Tallulah because, in a way, they were two sides of the same coin, two rebels without causes. But before you could even try your callused hand at matchmaking, Tallulah had shoulder checked you in the lunch line and started hollering about the starting pitcher on the baseball team asking her to the dance. You'd just nodded along like you always do.

Outside the gym is a payphone that no one's used in five years. Once the school finally got cell service, it became nothing more than a spot for boys to smoke weed. But tonight, it is your savior.

With stiff fingers, you slip two quarters out of your shoe and dial the number of the local McDonald's—you've had it memorized since infancy. The phone rings for a second before someone answers.

"McDonald's," they say in a voice resembling a croaking toad. "What do you want?"

"I need to speak to Colton," you say. "Tell him it's his sister."

The person on the other end of the call doesn't respond, but in about thirty seconds you hear Colton's voice.

"Hey, you," he says in his smooth country accent. He's always sounded a lot classier than everyone else. "Ain't you supposed to be at the dance?"

"I am at the dance," you say. "Come pick me up."

Colton sighs. "Come on, sister. I thought you said you'd try this time."

"I did try," you insist. "I stayed for an hour. And it was a shit hour, because Isaiah's in there putting his tongue down that girl's throat and MawMaw made me wear this god-awful dress that makes me look like a sack with a bird's nest for a head."

Colton doesn't say anything.

"Colt, *come on*," you plead.

He sighs. "I get off in fifteen."

"Thank you."

"Thank God, not me," Colton says. Then he hangs up, leaving you more grateful for your brother than you've ever been.

It's nearly ten when Colton finally pulls up in Pappy's old truck. In your waiting, you'd resorted to fishing the pins out of your stiff-as-a-board hairdo, only to have it not move an inch. You curse Miss Gladys under your breath, too angry to care that wishing a spinster woman ill would probably send you straight to Hell with all the dirty dancers.

Pins clutched in your fist, you hobble over to the truck feeling a confusing mix of gratitude and hatred. He leans out the driver's seat window in his McDonald's uniform. He's nineteen, nearly twenty, but still a senior in high school since he got held back in kindergarten because he couldn't even read the word "dog."

"Howdy," he says, smiling the faint smile he uses on you when he knows you're mad. "You sure you don't want to go back in there?"

You give him a look like fire and brimstone. Even though Colton still can't read a lick, he's smart enough to know when you aren't to be trifled with.

"All right then," he says, and you hop into the truck.

The left side gives a bit when you sit down, probably because one of the tires was stolen off a small abandoned tractor.

Colton considers you for a moment.

"Your hair sure does look like a bird's nest," he says.

You want to say something mean back, but your mind is too fried to think of anything. Instead, you just stick your tongue out like you're five years old again.

"I got you some fries," he says and nods to the brown paper bag sitting on the dashboard in front of you. Now you have to keep your mouth shut, especially because you've got MawMaw's voice in your head lecturing you about gratefulness.

"I'm sorry you missed your last spring formal," you say in between fries.

Colton shrugs as if it's nothing. You know it isn't nothing, because Colton's been working late every night since his sophomore year and never got to have a scrap of fun because of it.

"You can be upset about it, you know," you say. Colton just shrugs again and puts the truck in reverse. You drop the topic, knowing that Colton is as closed off as MawMaw's secret medicine drawer when it comes to his feelings.

As the two of you drive off, you spot Tallulah by herself outside the gym. She looks beautiful, clad in a sparkly navy-blue dress, dyed black hair swept over one shoulder. Her raccoon makeup is even more intense than usual, and she has silver glitter dusting her cheekbones. She's sitting on the pavement where you just were, head down with her tall, pointy heels in hand. You know she came with a boy, but now, she is alone. You feel a twinge of concern for her, and strangely, a bit of guilt for leaving.

If you had still been out there, she would have talked to you. Most people would have simply ignored you, maybe made note of dead Bubba's niece outside the dance by herself. You're starting to realize that Tallulah isn't most people.

Beyond the lights and music of the school is the darkness and silence typical of Ass Crack after nightfall. Usually, you find it calming, but tonight is different. Something about the black void past Colton's headlights unsettles you to your very core so, you rip your eyes away from the windows and stare at your shoes instead.

The radio plays the country music of your childhood, wailing songs about the girls who got away and the boys who drink to forget. You and Colton sit in a sort of reverent quiet, both lost in your own thoughts as the truck bounces over potholes and cracks.

"What do you think of that Tallulah girl?" you blurt, the navy sequins of her dress lingering in your mind.

"Well," Colton sighs. "I know the Reverend hates her almost as much as he hates all of Ma's kids."

You can't see Colton's wonky left ear from the passenger seat, but you know it's there. How could you, or anybody, ever forget it?

"She's in my Bible class," you say. "She sits in the back with me and the alleged homosexual since the Reverend can't stand to look at us."

Colton shakes his head. "It's bull."

"He made me run laps in the gym the other day because he saw me nod at Colby Jackson in the hallway. He said I have a Jezebel spirit."

Colton grits his teeth. "I know I shouldn't say this about a man who's my...father, but he is a false god if I've ever seen one."

You're dead silent. This is the first time you've ever heard Colton acknowledge his real daddy.

He continues, "He does all that preaching, then goes off shacking up with young girls and leaving them with babies to take care of."

Shacking up. Maybe there's a shack where people go to get babies.

Colton tightens his grip on the wheel. "Two babies, if you're our poor Ma."

So, your Ma had been to the Reverend's shack at least twice if she got both Colton and Isaiah out of it.

"Did he show up when you were born?" you ask, fiddling with your Walmart necklace.

Colton nods. "Showed up right after and told Ma to never tell anyone who my father is. Did the same thing when Isaiah came ten months later. Surely did the same thing to all the other girls he left with babies and..." He trails off, but soon enough his voice gets strong again. "And all my other half siblings."

"How'd you know all of this?"

"MawMaw told me one night after she had too many Bud Light's."

"Sounds like MawMaw."

Colton chuckles. "You know, I'm lucky I look like Ma for the most part. I don't think she'd like me as much as she does if I favored the Reverend as much as Isaiah."

Even in Isaiah's squirrely sort of face, those hellfire eyes are hard to ignore.

"The Reverend's a bad man," you say with more conviction than you've ever said anything in your life. "If I had a choice, I'd never set foot in his church again or sit in his classroom for another minute. When you go to college, you'll never have to see him again, even though he is your real daddy."

Colton's silence is heavy, and you realize you've said something wrong.

"Don't say all that," he says softly.

"Why?"

"Because I ain't going to college. I ain't ever leaving here and that's the way it's gonna be."

You're confused. "But Colt, all your money—"

He cuts you off. "It's for Isaiah and you."

You feel something rise in your throat. Suddenly, the high collar of MawMaw's dress is choking you. The truck grows stuffy with emotion. You swear you can see it beading on the surface of the windshield.

"Colt, are you...no, you can't," you stammer. "I won't take it, and Isaiah won't either." The intensity of the moment makes your accent flare up, your "can't" turning into "cain't" and all annunciation gone to shit.

"You will, 'cause I'm gonna make you." Colt says this like it's nothing. Like it's just fact, like someone wrote it in the Bible two thousand years ago. But this isn't nothing. It's the future. Shit on a stick, it's *your* future.

"I won't," you say again. "You're smart enough for college, even if it's Delta Community College. Colt, don't play like this."

"I'm not playin'. I can barely string two sentences together at nineteen and some change so, college sure as hell ain't for me. But you and Isaiah been in the honors classes since birth and I'm not gonna let y'all waste all that I didn't get."

You feel tears beginning to bead in your eyes. Thank God MawMaw said mascara was for whores and didn't let you wear any.

"Don't you worry none about your big brother, you hear?" Colton says. "I'll go train as an electrician or a plumber or something. I promise I won't be working at McDonald's forever."

You don't have words. You rarely have words, but this is different.

"And it's not like I've got both your tuition saved up or nothing. But with loans and scholarships and maybe two years at the community college...I think it'll help a bit."

"The Reverend," you gasp out. "We'll blackmail him and make him pay for you, too."

Colton looks at you like you're talking shit, but you aren't, not for one minute.

"I'm serious. I'll get something on him."

Colton shakes his head, solemn and resigned. "A 'man of God' like him is above the law. Ain't nothing we can do to him in this town."

"That's bullshit." You're feeling a confusing mix of seething, brokenhearted, and an emotion most foreign to you—hope.

Colton shrugs. "I never said it wasn't bullshit. It's just the way this little world works."

That's the best description of Ass Crack you've ever heard. This is a place that operates on its own set of rules, where leaving is akin to taking off in a rocket ship to outer space.

After a pause, Colton says, "It's not like I'm gonna make you go. But I know you want to. That's why I started saving the money."

You shake your head and do nothing to stop the tears from flowing down your cheeks. Your head is full of thoughts and a dizzy flutter of relief that you can't quite comprehend.

"Colt," you choke out. "That dance was so horrible." It's all you can think to say.

He laughs, low and Southern like he always does. It's his real laugh, not the tinny fake one he uses on folks in the McDonald's drive-through.

"They always are."

Your Ma's place is just as you left it, a bit ramshackle and worn down but still possessing a certain charm. It's just a squat three-bedroom house with yellow siding and peeling shutters framing the few windows. Two scraggily bushes sit beneath those windows, the extent of your Ma's gardening abilities. A sunken porch frames the front door, built by Colton and your Daddy one summer when you were a child.

You remember sitting in a plastic baby pool full of lukewarm water and watching them knock each board into place. Your father had been swearing up a storm and sweating bullets while the all too familiar Mississippi heat raged. As for Colton, he'd been silent and peaceful, content to wield a hammer and help his father. Perfect, as always. Of course, Isaiah had run off somewhere to avoid working, a habit he would carry into his teenage years. You'd stayed to watch for two reasons: you were a girl, so you would never be asked to help, and you'd loved being anywhere Colton was. Even as you got older and crankier, that never truly changed.

Colton gets out of the truck with his typical country boy swagger, leaving you alone for a moment. You stare at the house. You haven't been back since Ma effectively kicked you out, something you're starting to understand. She just doesn't like you.

Colton turns around to look at you, his red polo gone askew.

You know you've got to go inside. You really don't want to. But then you think about your perfect brother and the money.

You get out of the truck.

The two of you cross the porch in silence. The night air is warm, but not as warm as it could be. Colton's boots thump against the worn planks. Your bare feet against the dusty wood are reminiscent of your childhood in this house and all the splinters you could never dig out of your skin. Dangling from your fingertips, your good church heels clack against each other.

Colton doesn't knock. He just turns the doorknob and walks right in.

At the sight of the living room, you are struck with one thought.

It's different.

Your Ma got rid of the peeling fake leather couch you spent your childhood on and replaced it with something navy and lumpy. The walls have been painted a lighter shade of yellow and the rug is new. You're struck with a particularly awful thought. This is a room Uncle Bubba will never see.

Your Daddy is nowhere to be found, probably fast asleep by now, bone-tired from working construction. Not like he'd have much to say, even if he was here.

A part of you wants to leave, just turn your back and walk out the door. But you know you can't. Not when your Ma is standing at the kitchen table with a cigarette between her stiff fingers. Her eyes are just as tired as when you left.

"Hey Ma," you say and fold your arms around your midsection, suddenly self-conscious.

"Hi baby," she says. She looks you up and down, and a disappointed sort of smile spreads across her face. She sighs, drawn out and dramatic as always. "I really had hoped you'd turn out to be pretty. But the Lord doesn't always answer our prayers, does he?" And she takes another drag of her cigarette like she said nothing at all.

Out of the corner of your eye, you see Colton tense, but this isn't shit to you. You're a girl in the South. The faults of your body have always been just a casual discussion topic.

"Yeah, Ma," you say. "But the apple never did fall too far from the tree, did it?"

A few months ago, you wouldn't have said it. But it's today, and you just did.

Your Ma looks at you for a moment, as if she's seeing you for the first time. You: the terrible dress, your bird nest hair finally coming down around your shoulders, and the heels in your hand. You and all the shit lying inside that only Uncle Bubba, and sometimes Colton, bothered to unravel.

She looks at you and she says, "I suppose you're right, honey bun. Your father never was a looker."

You laugh coldly, something you never did before because you had to pretend like all this batshit crazy is normal. Yet, you're learning now that nothing in Ass Crack is typical. It's just another Mississippi town gone in circles until it swallowed itself.

You love your Ma something fierce, and that will never change, but you don't want to be her honey bun right now.

"Colt," you say. "Will you take me back home?"

HONKY
TONK
PEOPLE

The girls at school never pay much attention to you, hardly ever glancing your way. Probably because you're no good at most things and you've got the music taste of a middle-aged man.

Well, in all fairness—you'd like to be as fair as the county judge your Mawmaw calls "dumber than a headless chicken"—a good chunk of them girls don't have more than one eye. A lot of folks make it out of Home Ec. unscathed, but a lot of folks don't.

And the ones that do have two eyes, they like to honky tonk on the weekends, the weekdays, and during lunch period.

Really, they just like to honky tonk.

Colby Jackson leans over to you during the ~~Evolution~~ unit in biology class, bringing with him the scent of Dollar General deodorant. That Colby Jackson's always leaning, ever since the scoliosis hit and that city-slicker doctor down in Jackson put the rod in his back wrong. Now he can't play sports, even though he was half decent and the high school team always needs bodies. Still, he sure does a hell of a lot of pullups out in his garage. Your Mawmaw calls it "obscene and unholy," the way Colby Jackson's always showing off those corn-fed muscles of his in sleeveless shirts and sometimes no shirt at all. But the whole town knows that he's compensating for that wonky back and short left leg of his.

Colby Jackson's leaning is usually paired with some words from his mouth, though sometimes he does just lean, and most of them words are about cheap trucks, cheap beer, or other country song topics. You've started to realize that he talks like your Uncle Bubba, in the way that he always tells you stuff he isn't supposed to. Except Uncle Bubba was a hell of a lot smarter than Colby Jackson, who couldn't string together two sentences until the third grade. Yet, he never got held back, probably because none of the teachers could stand to teach his dumb ass again.

Last week, right in the middle of the ~~sexual reproduction~~ lecture, he'd said, "I just took the craziest piss. I think there was blood up in there."

Right now, he says, "You know what they say about them honky tonk women?"

You don't answer. You're not allowed to speak in biology class ever since you asked Coach Johnson where in the fresh hell storks were getting babies from.

Colby Jackson doesn't need you to answer. He's mostly deaf anyways—that city-slicker doctor did ear tubes, too.

"They say them honky tonk women are real eager for a roll in the hay, if you know what I'm sayin'."

You're starting to get it. Maybe hay rolling is where storks get babies from, and where boys get ahold of girls' flowers. A bit of pride blooms in your stomach.

Take that, Coach Johnson.

Your Uncle Bubba went to school with Coach Johnson and said he was dumb as a doornail and that he was a teacher because the school was the only place that would hire him after he did time for all that coke. You'd told your Uncle Bubba that you thought the government was real tyrannical if it could throw someone in jail just because they had a soda drinking problem. For some reason, Uncle Bubba had just laughed.

You give Colby Jackson a look like, *shut the hell up, boy*, but secretly you're grateful for this nugget of information. Finding out anything in Ass Crack is like that book your Uncle Bubba used to rant about, *1984.*

Colby Jackson just shrugs and grins as lopsided as his back. Your Ma says boys who grin like that are dangerous, but you don't think this one's smart enough to be dangerous.

The bell rings.

Over the past few weeks, you've taken to reading in the hallway between classes, mostly because it's easier to hide the Reverend-banned books the English teacher gives you behind your locker door. You've just finished *To Kill a Mockingbird*.

Now, you're real occupied with reading over the redacted Evolution unit of the biology textbook—you've just gotten into the ~~natural selection~~ portion—when you hear a sound like a truck starting. You don't look up. You've got a flashlight on the other side of the page so you can read the letters blacked-out by a cheap permanent marker. It takes a lot of concentration to decipher the sentences. Cars starting shouldn't distract your quest for knowledge. But you hear the sound again and finally look up.

Turns out it's just one of those honky tonk boys clearing his throat. He's looking just as he always does, dirty blond from the sun and regular dirty from everything else.

"Yeah?" you say, mostly because you're surprised that he's actually at school. Like you said, all they really do is honky tonk, and school isn't the ideal environment for those kinds of activities. You ought to know this boy—Ass Crack is a rather small town—but you can't place his face. You suppose you never were the most observant.

"Yeah," he answers.

"Well, spit it out."

"Come honky tonk with me and all them. It's the end of the year shindig," he says, but you know it's more of an order. Them honky tonk boys don't typically take no for an answer, especially when it comes to drinking. Still, you're wondering why he even asked you, since none of them party kids ever paid you much attention.

"What *is* a honky tonk?" you ask, because does anyone really know?

The only answer is a threatening gesture you dare not repeat.

You go honky tonk with them.

The only true-blue way to get to a honky tonk is in a pickup truck. Even so, you're starting to wish you'd just walked because the southern boy at the wheel is hitting every damn pothole in the road, sending your bony ass cracking against the poorly cushioned seats over and over again. And it doesn't seem like the A.C. is working either, because it's hotter than Hell in a handbasket.

You suppose you don't mind this environment too much. There's a country song about cornfield parties on the radio. You like country music. Everyone likes country music. The ones who say they don't are only trying to be different.

You turn to the southern boy driving. Honestly, you aren't sure if he's a boy. You strain your eyes for some sign of age. He could be either sixteen or forty. Bowl cuts are ageless.

"Has anyone ever *actually* had a party in a cornfield?" you ask him, because he seems like the type that would know.

His stare is blank, like you're not even there.

And—thank God—you've finally made it to the honky tonk.

All the girls have got their shoulders showing and their hair brushing the red dirt ground. The shorts are short, and the boots are dusty. Hell, Colby Jackson is gonna be so jealous.

It's in a field. Of course, it's in a field.

Fields aren't pretty, but this one's especially ugly, all trampled and dead from the partying and hay-rolling they've been doing all this time without ever inviting you. Trees surround the field like the fence of a pasture, closing all the troublemaking kids in one place and creating some sort of alcoholic chickencoop. Their old beer cans are strewn about like another tornado blew through, and the air is hazy from all the cigarettes smoke. The sun is starting to fade, sinking below the tree line—all pine, of course—casting the honky tonk in momentary golden light.

Now you feel silly for asking that Southern boy about cornfield parties. And you're not quite dressed for the occasion, that much is becoming obvious. You've got on Colton's old jeans with no belt, leaving them hanging loose around your belly button, paired with your Uncle Bubba's Third Eye Blind t-shirt. Most of your clothes are hand-me-downs from those two because your Ma couldn't stand to part with most of her teenage clothes. Some kind of nostalgia she didn't want you tainting.

But as silly and underdressed as you are, you're still here. Tallulah's probably somewhere on the fringes of this hot mess—this seems like her kind of place. You scan the crowd for dark hair, but you can't find her. She's probably out in the woods with a boy who thought they were going out there to smooch explaining the plot of that Reverend-banned vampire book you'd managed to get her.

The "all them" the honky tonk boy mentioned are here, too. They're looking like they always do around town and in school (when they decide to go), clad in work boots, roughed up jeans, and baseball hats just perched on their heads like birds. Your Pappy used to say to keep away from birds because they're "the Devil's watchmen."

But these birds...these birds have got wings you want, wings that could pick you up and take you somewhere else.

Somewhere.

With big buildings and new people and wild mystery and—

"You there," says one of the honky tonk women. "Quit thinkin', start drinkin'."

She's got a point. And she's beautiful. She's got two moss green eyes and has split ends that get caught under the soles of your feet. You can't help but think that she's one of the girls God took His time with.

In her hand is a beer. "The Devil's elixir," your MawMaw likes to say.

But MawMaw ain't here.

That's all you say to yourself as the beer goes down like water, brown as the silt the Mississippi River kicks up.

That's all you say to yourself as the world starts spinning faster and the music gets louder and the honky tonk woman has her callused hand in yours.

That's all you say to yourself as you start to wonder who you are, if you can do this, if you're even your Ma's daughter and Colton's sister.

That's all you say to yourself as the blue lights start flashing and sirens holler like the mourners at Uncle Bubba's funeral.

But you're having a hell of a good time. The sirens are far away, calling you to smash your boat and your skull on the rocks; yet, you are immune, dancing and drenched in sweat. You aren't very good at dancing but you're realizing that it all boils down to hair tossing, wiggling, and spinning around those heart wrenching girls. You understand why the honky tonk kids do this, now. Because you've forgotten most of the terrible things in your life, and you can almost pretend that Uncle Bubba is alive, and you are radiant like the honky tonky women. You're so euphoric that you're starting to wish they'd invited Colby, though all this dancing would probably mess up his back, maybe send the rod straight into his brain.

"MawMaw ain't here," you say to yourself as you let the music take you over.

You're starting to understand why the Reverend is so against drinking and dancing. Who needs God when you can find religion at the bottom of a beer bottle and in the whine of an electric guitar?

"MawMaw ain't here!" you holler because you've tasted freedom and you ain't gonna be the same.

"MAWMAW AIN'T HERE!"

"Goddamnit y'all, the cops are!" says the honky tonk woman. All the sudden she's running with her hand still in yours, dragging you like the dead weight you are. Dead weight, dead ends, and all those questions you ask in biology class, but they won't answer. Just leave you hanging like Uncle Bubba, leave you quiet and scared and running drunk from the cops that all know your MawMaw from church.

And, oh Lord, you're crashing. The high was dangerous, you should've known, because everything that comes up must come down. You'd read that in the redacted part of the Law of Gravity unit using a flashlight and your sharp eyes. Coach Johnson said Isaac Newton was "an atheist liar who knew not the Truth of God". You're not sure if that's true, but you don't care, because you thwarted Coach Johnson's dumbass with that flashlight of yours and the mind your Uncle Bubba cultivated.

When the honky tonk woman's fingers slip from yours, you don't really blame her. She hauled your ass this far; you know that analogy with Jesus and the beach. But she's not the Son of God, just a Delta woman like any other.

And now you're here, and you're alone.

Out here, the pine trees grow in razor straight lines. It's another question you asked a long time ago. *Why're all them pine trees in lines?* And nobody answered.

No one answered, and you sat through the service—the screaming, singing, and sweating all for Jesus's sake.

MawMaw never let you lay down in the pews at church. So down you lay now, down into the pine needles. From the ground, the trees are taller than anything you've seen before, taller than the tallest buildings in Jackson. They could so easily take you.

Then it hits you like a summer storm.

The trees are in straight lines because someone planted them here.

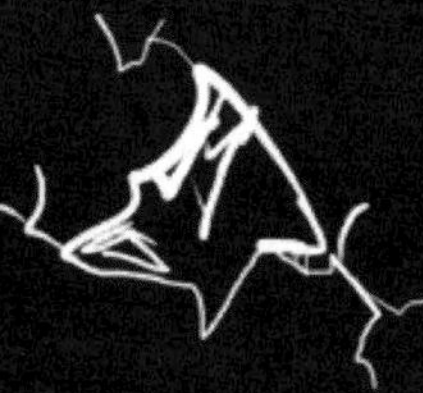

A LETTER FOR YOU

You're about three hours from home, even farther into nowhere than Ass Crack.

But it's still the Delta. It's still Mississippi. Sometimes it seems like everything is.

You call this place Butt Hole, just a little bit worse than the Crack. It's the kind of place you only go for your brothers' football games because you, your Ma, and MawMaw can hitch a ride on the team bus, an old yellow school bus that holds the familiar smell of ancient fake leather and the reek of teenage boys. Your spot, right in the front next to MawMaw, was dusty when you sat down. This bus is always dusty no matter how much sweeping Isaiah does in lunchtime detention. The cheerleaders in the back complain about it, and you don't blame them because the short skirts of their uniforms are bright white. We can't have the pride and joy of Ass Crack High showing up to every away game with dusty stains right on their bottoms. Your Ma had wanted you to be a cheerleader, but your MawMaw vetoed it, saying that cheerleading is only for tramps and Jezebels.

The Butt Hole High football field isn't much more than dead grass and some wooden bleachers on the home side. As for the visitors, y'all get a bench and maybe take a trip to the concession stand for some nachos.

Though you've never been here, this place feels familiar. You think that's because you understand the importance of a small-town football field. It's a place to go on Friday night when there's shit else to do the rest of the week, other than church on Sunday. There's an air of excitement that surrounds these poorly kept football fields, a hope that something semi-interesting might happen tonight. Maybe the team will win, some PTA ladies will get into a hollering match, or two heathen teenagers will light a joint under the bleachers. No matter what, it'll be something to talk about in a world where the same three topics are discussed anytime the church ladies have their luncheons.

This week they'll surely talk about how the Ass Crack boys are on the football field getting their rear ends kicked by those even more country boys. Each hit of their offensive line shatters bones and knocks brains around skulls. You see Isaiah go flying a few times and Colton barely holding his own. You're not too worried, because both have had more concussions than the bird that likes to fly into the window of MawMaw's trailer.

Some of them Butt Hole boys have full beards and barrel chests wider than the Mississippi River. And, of course, they've been eyeing all you out-of-town girls as you mosey to the concession stand during halftime. "Fresh tail," they call y'all as you walk past the field. You mouth back that humans don't have tails and that they ought to stop hitting each other so hard before they get even slower in the head. They just laugh at you, but it doesn't bother you too much because you've gotten used to boys laughing at you.

You're walking with Colby—who isn't on the football team on account of his wonky skeleton, but they let him be a water boy—when all the Butt Hole boys start hollering at you. You don't understand why they're wolf-whistling at you in particular since you're wearing a Delta State Fighting Okra t-shirt and bangs your MawMaw cut far too short. You wouldn't exactly call it an appetizing look.

"Wanna take a ride on a real man, baby?" one of them shouts. "I can show you something much bigger than that lopsided son of a bitch over there can."

Colby lifts his head like he wants to say something to them, but you tell him to pipe down.

"Why should I?" he says, fiddling with his Mississippi Braves ballcap. Under the brim, his face is twisted with disgust.

You give him a look. "Because I said so and I'm the one they're acting like that over. Plus, my MawMaw don't like me talking to you, so I can't have you drawing attention to the fact I'm disobeying her."

He grunts. "It just ain't right the way they're acting."

"You think I don't know that?" you scoff. And then you do something you've never done before. You give those wolf-whistling, good-for-nothing boys the bird. Adrenaline burns hot in your veins as you tell that

Southern Belle bullshit to fuck off. No pretending. Not anymore. Uncle Bubba wouldn't want you to tolerate this, any of it.

Colby looks at you in shock, but somewhere in his odd-looking face you see a glimpse of admiration.

"Good job," he says after a beat. You suppress a faint smile.

You continue in silence for a moment, Colby's lurching steps falling in time with yours.

"Why do you disobey your MawMaw?" he asks suddenly.

"What?"

"I mean, why do you talk to me when she don't like it?"

"I don't know," you say, but that's a lie. It's not the kind of thing you want to admit to that Jackson boy, because he brings out your pride like no one else. But, shit, you've got nothing left to lose, not after your Uncle Bubba kicked it.

"Maybe it's because you're the only one who will—talk to me, that is."

"You're the only one who will talk to me either," says Colby.

You feel strange acknowledging it, but, in a way, you've become friends with Ole Colby Jackson ever since he came over and bothered you that day in the snow. He makes you wonder if MawMaw was wrong, because he's never stolen any flowers from you, never even tried. The petunias you planted this past spring have remained untouched in the flower bed, healthy as ever, except when the damn deer get to them.

"Most of those boys," you gesture to the boys on the football field, "they're shitheads. They think they can act like that because this is Mississippi and they're boys."

Colby nods all solemn. In a faint voice, he says, "This can be a hard place to be."

The two of you fall into silence. It's a hot night, stuffier than an old school Southern Baptist. Sweat runs down your forehead, stinging your eyes and plastering your hair to your face. You don't feel beautiful. You don't really feel like a person if you're honest. A part of you, one that is larger than you'd like to admit, wonders if this is the way Uncle Bubba felt before he died. And you wonder if the same force that pulled him into the piney woods is calling to you now.

"Is," you say.

"What?"

"I'm correcting you. This *is* a hard place to be."

Colby stops dead in his tracks, his scuffed-up cowboy boots screeching to a halt. The floodlights cast harsh shadows over the misshapen planes of his face, and he stares at you so intensely that you're tempted to shrink beneath his gaze. Though it's not Hallmark movie pre-kissing intense; no, it's something they don't put on TV because it doesn't quite make sense. You think you should say something, yet you don't. You just stare right back.

"I can't believe you said that," he says.

You start to turn red, start to make excuses, but he cuts you off.

"I didn't think anyone else felt the same way."

His words do confusing things to the rhythm of your breathing—slow, all of a sudden, despite your heart beating fast. You don't know what to say because, even now, you don't want to have anything in common with that riff raff Jackson boy who listens to Irish rock and wears hats crooked on his blond head. He's an outcast. He's a leper. That's what people used to call Uncle Bubba when he was alive.

If you are like Colby Jackson, it means two things.

You're an outcast. *You're* a leper.

The truth is you've always known this, but it was easier before Uncle Bubba died. Now that he's gone, the whole town is just waiting for you to follow him. Bubba's oddball niece who's never been called sweet or pretty or anything condescendingly nice because none of those good words were ever true for you. Something about you makes them heartbreakingly honest. They reveal a truth that's been there since before you could shoot a gun.

It's easy to see that they expect you to die disgraced like Bubba, and that they expect the same from Colby. MawMaw's been trying to keep you out of Hell, but they know she's failing. You know she's failing.

This is a hard place to be.

The team bus leaves you at Butt Hole High School.

They roll off while you're dumping out the orange Gatorade cooler behind the chain link fence surrounding the endzone. Your MawMaw's had you doing odd jobs for the football team since middle school, though they still manage to forget. You hear the whine of smooth tires over the clatter of nearly melted ice sloshing around in hose water. When you turn, you see the bus pulling out of the parking lot. Oddly enough, you feel no despair over them leaving you high and dry in the worst part of Mississippi. Instead, there's a distinct ache of emptiness, maybe something closer to resignation.

You drop the cooler, muttering halfhearted curses. You're not surprised they left you. They've done it before at other football games, but never ones quite so far from home. Maybe Colton will notice, even with all those concussions, and have them turn the bus around. You can imagine exactly how he'd say it, too. He'd march right up to the bus driver and say in a voice both polite and firm, "My sister isn't here. Please go back and get her."

This is all wishful thinking. Colton's probably snoring against the window while Isaiah flirts with the cheerleaders. MawMaw won't notice you're gone until tomorrow morning, and Ma won't notice at all. The only person you have left is Colby, and he's not the kind of boy you can count on to be observant. Tallulah would have noticed, but she's been banned from away games ever since the Reverend accused her of distracting the Ass Crack team with her "womanly wiles".

You sit there on the ground for a while, watching the residents of Butt Hole slowly start to leave for their homes or make-out parking lots. No one has noticed that you don't belong here. You suppose you blend in well, just another redneck girl with a Delta face and a farm-strong figure.

You're beginning to accept that no one's coming back for you, and there's a fat chance that any of these Butt Hole hicks have a cell phone you could call your Daddy on.

You're realizing that you only have two options: sit there forever or get back home somehow.

So, you start walking.

It's dark out, and you're not really sure where you're going, but you think this is a street you might have come down. So, that's where you walk. It's just a typical Mississippi highway, riddled with potholes to the point you're not sure it could even be called a road anymore. The only light guiding your way is the waning moon. It washes over you with its cold, pale glow.

It's hot. It's so goddamn hot, and you can't stop thinking. Your mind is a twister, strong as the tornado that destroyed the town last spring. That's the problem with you, you suppose. You've got a destructive way of being.

Despite the moon, the road is nearly pitch black. You should be afraid, but you're not. You've got too much occupying your mind to be afraid. Inside you swims Ole Colby Jackson's lopsided face, your Ma the day she kicked you out, Tallulah in that navy dress, and Colton's money. Truly, it's mostly the money that occupies you. Thinking about it all piled up in the bank—probably no more than a few hundred dollars, but there all the same—makes you sick to your stomach. All those shifts at McDonald's, all those lawns mowed, all those fields weeded. Just for you and Isaiah.

A cloud blocks out the moon, dropping you into complete darkness like the inside of Uncle Bubba's coffin.

You find yourself on your knees on the shoulder of the highway, sweating bullets and wanting to cry. The blades of grass live up to their name, digging into your skin and surely leaving deep red imprints.

You could scream if you wanted to. No one would hear you.

Every part of your body hurts at the thought, but you know what you've got to do.

"I can't take that money," you say into the dark pines. The trees understand. They're even more stuck than you.

This is the worst you've felt in a while. That money you'll never touch. That money that will have to go to Isaiah and his rebellious brilliance. You're not a rebel, not really; you just can't do anything right. But you can't leave Colton and MawMaw and Tallulah and Isaiah and Colby and all you've ever known, no matter how shit it is.

This is what the Reverend would tell you to do if you'd been dumb enough to come to him for council. "This is your home, girl," he would say. "God wants you to stay." Then he would tell you to take your clothes off, just he's told all those other girls over the years, and you'd end up doing whatever it is that gives women children. Billy didn't say it at the funeral, but that's why Uncle Bubba stopped going to church.

He told you that once while he was drunk off his ass. "You're my niece," he'd said, slurring his words and looking at you with half closed eyes. "And I worry about you. Stay away from the Reverend and keep your clothes on if you have to be near him. He liked your Ma once, and he'd do what he did to her to you if he got a chance. Make him hate you, baby. Be a heathen, my girl. It's what you've got to do to keep safe in this God forsaken town."

At that memory, you finally let out a scream.

You're banging on the ground with your fists, like some sort of cavewoman anguishing before words were invented. This is a pain beyond language. Clovers and wildflowers crack under your strength, muscles built up by generations of crop picking and plowing fields, a hardness you can't escape.

You won't escape. That's how it's going to be.

The moon returns, casting your kneeling shadow across a grove of Queen Ann's Lace.

That's where the mailman finds you, curled up among the white flowers waiting for Uncle Bubba.

You're not dead yet, but he thinks you are at first. You don't move when you hear his mail truck stop on the side of the road and tentative footsteps make their way towards you. He nudges you with his foot. You stay still, hoping he'll just go away. He doesn't. He presses his rough fingers to your neck, searching for a pulse. When he unfortunately finds one, he lets out a sigh of relief.

"Ma'am," he says. "Would you get up please?"

You keep your eyes shut and stay silent. The grass and flowers are cool against your skin. What a perfect place to stay forever.

"Ma'am," he says again. Maybe his strategy is to simply annoy you into submission. You keep your eyes shut and your head tucked into your chest, even as you feel your Delta woman temper begin to flare.

"Ma'am."

"What?" you snap, taking the bait, but staying determinedly on the ground.

"I'm just checking if you're alright."

"What do you think, buddy?"

"Are you hurt?"

"Not physically."

"I see," he says, shuffling his feet awkwardly. "But you can't lay here forever, miss. You gotta get up eventually."

"I can do whatever the hell I want. Ain't nothing to lose now. Not that you'd understand."

The mailman sighs. "Ma'am, I'm a government employee. I understand more than your young self can know." He grabs your arm. "Now get up. I'm taking you back to wherever you come from."

You finally open your eyes. It's still dark out, and there's a white mail truck parked on the side of the road. The mailman is of the typical stock, a bit overweight with a beard like Santa Claus. You're still limp, but he hauls you onto your unsteady feet.

"Where are you from?" he asks.

In your mind, you hear MawMaw's rants about strange men. This man is probably going to kill you.

"Ass Crack, Mississippi," you answer anyways.

"Well, ain't it convenient that that's where I'm heading."

You grunt in response and rip your arm out of the mailman's grasp. The Queen Ann's Lace whispers to you, pleading with you to come back and wait for Uncle Bubba. Yet, something makes you move. You think it might be the survival instinct within you that refuses to die despite how much you want to.

You're well aware that getting in this truck is a terrible, unsafe idea, but what is life but a series of terrible, unsafe ideas?

The mailman, who you notice has sort of hazy quality to him, opens the passenger door of the mail truck for you—a typical Southern man. Running about telling women what to do every day of the week, but at least they'll hold the door for you.

"Thank you," you mutter because Southern manners persist even on the side of the road.

The mail truck is crowded with bundles of letters, of course, and cardboard boxes wrapped in packing tape.

When the mail man climbs into the driver's seat, you say, "I didn't know this many people still wrote letters." You feel like death walking, but you know you ought to talk to this man—Southern politeness and all. He is giving you a—hopefully—free ride home.

The mail man's haze seems to grow as he sits there. You can almost see right through him, your eyes picking out the blue veins beneath his skin. You've never seen a man so pale, at least not in Ass Crack where people are tanned from the Mississippi sun and a heritage they'll never admit to. It's almost frightening, that paleness, like the moon above you.

"They don't," says the mail man as he puts the truck into drive and it takes off with a lurch. "Most of those letters are my own."

"Oh," you say as the motor rumbles down the road. You look behind you and find letters scattered in floorboard. "Who are you writing to?"

The mail man shrugs. "Whoever will read them." He turns to look you directly in the face. It makes your skin crawl. "And whoever needs them."

"So, you're a writer?" you say.

"I wouldn't go that far. I'm just a person who writes."

You curl your fingers into a fist. The joints are starting to ache. "My Uncle Bubba was a writer."

You've never said that out loud before.

"He never called himself a writer either," you continue. "Just someone who writes."

The mailman considers you for a moment, then puts the mail truck into park. "I suppose you're the right person then," he says.

You're pretty sure this is where you die, gutted by some mail man on the side of the road because the team bus left you in Butt Hole, Mississippi. A fitting way to go for a girl like you.

You stay seated as he hops out of the truck and opens up the back doors. You hear him riffling through all the mail, muttering to himself as he does. Then he makes an affirmative sound and a sharp edge presses into your throat. No, it isn't a knife. It's the crisp fold of an envelope.

"For you," the mailman says.

You take the letter, noting how pristine it is. Bright white paper with *Bubba's Niece/ My Third Cousin, Ass Crack, Mississippi,* printed on it in dark blue pen.

"What?" you say, but you instantly know who this is from. The return address is *Jackson*, nothing else. You whip your head around.

"How did you get this? How did you know?"

The mailman has climbed back in the driver's seat by now. "I told you," he says, those wide eyes boring into you. "Whoever needs them."

You're scared to open it. But he's right. You need it.

You open the letter slowly, breaking the adhesive with great care. The stickiness clings to the pads of your fingers, tinted green by clovers and flower stems. Inside is a piece of paper covered in Willie Joe's neat handwriting. There is no introduction. Just a poem.

Come find me on the levee.
Smile with that writer's mouth.
Let the river hold fast.
Let me stay away.
But know I love you.

And that the pine forest.
It would have been my destiny.
Strung up like you.
From the lowest branch of a
Tall, skinny pine.
And buried at the crossroads.

Go.
I'm talking to you.
In you is Bubba's heart.
Which means you need to run.
Or you'll burn yourself alive like him.

Bring his ghost with you.
Cut him down from the tree.

Silence. Just your slow pulse thrumming in your head.

You hold the poem against your heart and stare into the pine trees. They know. They know you know, and that you can't admit it to yourself, or you'll die like Bubba. But they whisper to you, those pines, the needles rubbing together like fingers against a banjo. Between the dark lines of the forest, you can almost see it: your Uncle Bubba hanging from the lowest limb of a smooth trunked pine tree.

He killed himself last summer, then you buried him at the crossroads in the heat of the Devil's armpit. You wore MawMaw's old black dress to the funeral and ruined it with your sweat and the tears that wouldn't flow.

Uncle Bubba was a lot like you. Now everyone in Ass Crack, Mississippi is waiting for you to die like he did.

But they won't ever say what happened. They lie sweet Southern lies, spinning up tales that he drowned, or burned, or seized until he was fried from the inside out. Only the trees have been honest to you.

Your Uncle Bubba killed himself.

And you are afraid that you will follow his boot tracks into the pine forest—all the way down to Hell.

CATFISH
POND
WOMAN

There are ponds in the Mississippi Delta.

You find yourself there when you've wrecked the car again, grumbling that it wasn't your fault, when of course it was. That deer hadn't come out of nowhere—you'd gone hunting for that deer in MawMaw's old Nissan. You're coming off an emotional hangover, too, full of burnt coffee and youth.

These ponds are perfect circles, crisp lines in overgrown earth.

Before you unlearned the word "why," you used to ask just that.

In response, they say there are catfish in there. But they say it in a distinctly uncatfish-like way. See, it's all in the twist of their faces, the grimace when they force the words. And the pain of it all makes them sound Northern, like they're masking their accents for the IRS man on the phone.

The ways of the catfish are blatant, easy. Those fish know when they're fixin' to be fried, but they don't run—no legs. So, it's easy for you to know that it's not catfish in these ponds.

And yeah, the sight coming from beneath the muddy depths doesn't really shock you.

Everybody warns you ‘bout those Mississippi women, and if you are one, they warn you about yourself.

They never did say nothing about catfish pond women.

She crawls out of the pond heaving, clutching finfulls of soft red dirt. Her webbed hands crush Queen Ann’s Lace beneath their weight, stems snapping and crunching. Her hair’s a bit tangled, but she’s pretty, aside from the gray of her skin and the whiskers catty-corner to her mouth.

You feel a hint of satisfaction, because there sure weren’t catfish in there, unless this lady counts.

When she opens her jaws, showing nearly toothless gums, you should be afraid, but you aren’t. And your instincts are right to trust her, because she seems to be a real straight talking catfish pond woman.

“Got a light?” she rasps, voice like a dirt road.

You say “yeah,” and toss her the red lighter you carry around because your MawMaw smokes a twelve-pack a day but can’t be bothered to carry her own damn light.

“How long you been smoking?” you ask, making gas-station-bathroom-type conversation.

“I don’t,” she says and swallows the lighter whole. “Don’t really care for the nicotine.”

“I don’t either.” You make a mental note to swing by the Dollar General and get a new lighter, because MawMaw’s the type to whoop you if you haven’t got a light.

The catfish pond woman burps, then considers you for a moment. The considering makes you uncomfortable because it's a deeper kind of judgement than even the ladies at church do. Yeah, them church ladies are always looking for weed-red eyes or the cowlick in the dead center of your forehead, but it's nothing more than that surface-level, foot washing Baptist bullshit.

As for the catfish pond woman, she has these black eyes that seem to know nothing and everything all at once. They remind you of Uncle Bubba's eyes, *your* eyes. MawMaw used to say that the beady eyes the two of you share made for troublesome people, the pot-stirring kind of people who won't ever amount to nothing.

Finally, she speaks.

"Life gets better outside of this shit town."

"Yeah?" you answer, wanting to ask more, but your Uncle Bubba knew a guy who got drowned by a catfish.

"Yeah, kid. I got friends in the river, free as birds, except not really, 'cause they ain't got wings or legs."

You both sit in silence for a moment. It's an even heavier silence than the ones you're used to, which is a feat like the biblical plagues. Because in the Mississippi Delta, the air is heavy with all that's unsaid, all the years of crawfish fighting rings and tornadoes with the strength of demigods. All those years of living and dying and never leaving.

"Why're you still here, then?" you ask. It's probably a bad thing to ask even a catfish pond woman. Nobody likes to be asked why they never made it out.

"Ain't got a choice, baby. Hell, if I had one, I'd be out in the Gulf where the water tastes like salt and the beer's always good. But you're born where you're born and I got born in this damn pond, my own little slice of hell."

She looks at you in the way that only a catfish pond woman can. You think you might puke.

"It's a shit town," she repeats.

The words built up inside finally break your breastbone. Out they come, flowing brown and fast like that goddamn river.

"This town ain't just shit, it's *murderous*. It killed him and I'm *dying*, ma'am, I'm dying."

You feel tears pinprick your eyes. You don't cry much, especially not in front of new folks, but she, this catfish pond woman, feels like a safe space.

She speaks like it's the most obvious answer in the world.

"You got legs, baby. Just walk on out of this pond."

And the catfish pond woman slips into the deep.

End

Acknowledgements

First, I'd like to thank the team at Red Rook Press, especially Paul Albano and Anna Kate Baxter, for pouring their hearts and souls into this project and making my childhood dreams come true. Thank you for seeing the potential in my weird manuscript to become a weird book.

Thank you to all of the professors I've had at the University of Alabama. Whether you taught me biology, chemistry, or creative writing, you all have broadened my horizons.

Thank you to the Blount Scholars Program for bringing me my best college friends and putting me through academic hazing.

Thank you to the sisters of Alpha Omega Epsilon for supporting me throughout my academic career. Though we are a STEM focused sorority, you have all been beyond supportive of this book and my literary ambitions as a whole.

Thank you to everyone who has been a part of my life at the University of Alabama. Thank you for talking me in or out of my stupid ideas, and being there for me when it inevitably blows up in my face. Thank you for the late nights doing homework, watching bad movies, or just talking. There are too many of you to name, but you know who you are.

Thank you to my ride or dies, my Mississippi muses, Emmory Bridges, Cas Simpson, Abia Walker, and Leah Clark. Y'all are really my day ones and I'm forever lucky to have found such amazing best friends so early in life.

Of course, thank you to my family, both immediate and extended, for always supporting my love of reading and writing. Thank you to Auntie Em, Aunt Joanna, Lela, Lolo, Grandpa Bill, and Grandma Judy.

Thank you to my younger siblings, Stella and Evan, for never once providing me with peace and quiet, but always plenty of memories. I love you both very much (even if Stella can't remember the name of this book).

Thank you to my dad, Tim McCarty, for being the best dad anyone could be. Thank you for answering all of my childhood questions about outerspace and nuclear war. I love you.

Lastly, thank you to my mother, Michelle McCarty. I am thanking her last because had I put her first, she would never have made it to the end due to the amount of crying. You are surely crying now. Thank you for reading to me so much when I was a kid and instilling a love of literature in me. Thank you for being the only person who read my articles in The Bear Facts. Thank you for being an amazing mom. I love you.

About the author

Bianca McCarty is a poet and fiction writer from Madison, Mississippi. She is currently an undergraduate student at the University of Alabama majoring in Biology. Her poetry has been published in the Marr's Field Journal. In 2022, she received the Michael Dalton Goodson Memorial Prize in Poetry for her poem, "Father of Waters | Burning Mississippi." In her free time, she can be found working in her research lab, journaling, or taking walks with friends.

About the artists

Addie Dobereiner is an undergraduate at the University of Alabama.

• "Five and a Half Feet Under"

DeAndra Gauntt was born and raised in Montgomery, Alabama and is an undergraduate student at the University of Alabama. She is pursuing a BFA in Interdisciplinary Studies with a focus on Art Business. DeAndra's specialty lies in digital illustrations, focusing on character and environment storytelling, while also engaging in prose writing in the fantasy, science-fiction, drama, and romance genres. Much of her artwork and writing focuses on providing Black American representation in genres in which minorities are often underrepresented. In her free time, she enjoys sewing, reading, crafting, playing her favorite video games, and watching other people play her favorite video games.

• "Illegal Bible Class" •"Jackson Siren Call" • "Tornado Fishing"

Elizabeth Golembiewski grew up in Fenton, Michigan and is now a BFA Studio Art student at the University of Alabama. She concentrates in drawing and digital media, but she's also developing her skills as a sculptor. She prefers media such as pastels, bronze, and sticky tabs, where she can build up layers of rough texture. Impressionist art is one of her larger influences.

•cover •"The Money" • "A Letter for You"

Ainsley Greer grew up in Memphis, Tennessee and is currently a student at the University of Alabama pursuing a BFA in Graphic Design. While in college, she discovered her love for digital art and book designs. She has displayed her paintings in two galleries in Tuscaloosa: Wellness Walls for Art (2024) and First Friday Art Walk (2022).

•table of contents •"Dollar General"

Anna Luis is a creative media, English, history, and theatre major from South Carolina who is also working towards her MBA. She thrives on engaging with her diverse interests by creating in many mediums and can most often be found hanging around rescued street dogs. She plans to create films and television as a career. Vegan. Sleeps with the light on.

• "Snow" • "Kudzu Detention"

Anna White is an avid reader of poetry and fantasy works, with some of her favorites being Julie Kagawa's *Blood of Eden* series and various collections of folklore, classic fairy tales, and mythology. She loves to pet moss, and, similarly to certain birds, she adores shiny objects and things that go clink. Anna's life dream is to live in a cryptic yet luxurious cave with lots of beanbags, books, and RPG video games, of which Skyrim and Red Dead Redemption 2 are her all-time favorites.

•"Honky Tonk People" • "Catfish Pond Woman"

Red Rook Staff

Red Rook Press is a student-run literary press from the University of Alabama.

Acquisitions

Anna Kate Moorer (liaison), Anna Kate Baxter, Jane Champ-O'Connell, Claire Duke, Hannah French, Camryn Haag, Angie Henle, Aric Huffman, Sydney Jason, Vivian Johnson, Meghen Kellem, Alaina Kelley, McKenzie Knight, Olivia LaRose, Cassie Montgomery, Chance Phillips, Marin Poleshek, Erin See, Jordan Steele, John Underwood, Alyssa Walker, Alyssa Wallner

Audio

McKenzie Knight, Jordan Steele, Ever Wood

Content Editing

Anna Kate Baxter (liaison), Jack Armstrong, Jane Champ-O'Connell, Claire Duke, Hannah French, Camryn Haag, Alyssa Heitz, Emma Hurst, Kelsie Jackson, Olivia LaRose, Quade Mainzer, Kristie Meyer, Izzy Piper, Erin See, Zach Vinnola,Alyssa Walker, Alyssa Wallner

Design and Production

DeAndra Gauntt (liaison), Angie Henle, Addie Dobereiner, Michael Esparza, Hannah French, Ainsley Greer, Elizabeth Golembiewski, Anna Luis, Jordan Steele, Anna White

Promotions and Outreach

Maya Mungo (liaison), Martin Albright, Anna Kate Baxter, Camryn Haag, Sarah Vance Harrison, Kelsie Jackson, Jordana Kinder, Morinsola Kukoyi, Reese Johnson, Nic Lowery, Hannah Mauck, Cassie Montgomery, Jesse Mullins, Averi O'Brien, Erin See, Jordan Steele

Website Design and Content

Nic Lowery (liaison), Autumn Carpenter, Hayley Green, Aric Huffman, Meghan Kellem, McKenzie Knight, Anna Luis, Jesse Mullins, Ansel Smith, Jordan Steele

Faculty Advisers

Paul Albano, Merrill Lee Girardeau, Stephanie Marker, Jane Morton, Travis Turner

Note on Typography

This book is set in King's Caslon, a typeface originally designed by William Caslon in the 18th century. Elegant and precise, Caslon's fonts became well-known for their sophistication and quality, and his foundry dominated the printing industry in 1700s England. This modern interpretation of Caslon's style upholds its classic tradition while enhancing legibility for today's readers.

Page numbers, dropcaps, and headings are set in **Old Times American Heavy**, a typeface inspired by late 19th-century letterpress printing. Its historic yet gritty feel created by its decorative serifs and imperfect glyphs is reminscent of old pages and antique printing.